Taya noticed a la...
behind them.

"Um, Keegan. Think our friend from the bakery just happens to be going in the same direction as us?"

"Any other day, I'd say yes. Let's see if he keeps after us."

Keegan rounded the corner, and the pickup followed. The engine roared as it increased speed and gained on them. Taya's stomach lurched as the truck barreled into the back bumper.

Keegan reached into his jacket pocket and withdrew his phone, tossing it to Taya. "Call 9-1-1 and report a reckless driver. Give them the make, model and vehicle registration plate."

The truck moved closer, providing a better visual, but another thrust forced the phone from Taya's hand. It landed with a thud on the floorboards.

The pickup hit them again, throwing Taya into the dashboard. The SUV's tires screeched as the force sent her and Keegan swaying across the road and headed for a metal mile marker. They lacked horsepower to outrun the truck—and strength to prevent the driver from forcing them off the road...

Sharee Stover is a Colorado native transplanted to Nebraska, where she lives with her husband, three children and two dogs. Her mother instilled in her the love of books before Sharee could read, along with the promise, "If you can read, you can do anything." When she's not writing, she enjoys time with her family, long walks with her obnoxiously lovable German shepherd and crocheting. Find her at shareestover.com or on Twitter, @shareestover.

Books by Sharee Stover

Love Inspired Suspense

GRAVE
CHRISTMAS
SECRETS

SHAREE STOVER

LOVE INSPIRED SUSPENSE
INSPIRATIONAL ROMANCE

LOVE INSPIRED® SUSPENSE
INSPIRATIONAL ROMANCE

ISBN-13: 978-1-335-40318-6

Recycling programs for this product may not exist in your area.

Grave Christmas Secrets

For questions and comments about the quality of this book, please contact us at CustomerService@Harlequin.com.

Love Inspired
22 Adelaide St. West, 40th Floor
Toronto, Ontario M5H 4E3, Canada
www.Harlequin.com

Printed in U.S.A.

For thou art my lamp, O Lord:
and the Lord will lighten my darkness.
−2 Samuel 22:29

For my mom, who first introduced me to Jesus
and encouraged me to keep reading.
You inspired my faith and my love for books.

Acknowledgments

Many thanks to:

My editor, Emily Rodmell.

Dr. Brittany Walter and Brianna Petersen
for their expertise and kindness in
answering all of my research questions.

My critique group.

Most of all, thank You, Father God.
All glory and honor belong to You.

ONE

Three can keep a secret if two of them are dead. Forensic anthropologist Taya McGill disagreed with Benjamin Franklin's famous quote. In her experience, the dead were horrible secret keepers. Rather, she'd dub them mysterious pirates hoarding a treasure trove of clues. And as a general rule, far more reliable than most living people she'd encountered.

Taya cherished the incredible honor of speaking for the dearly departed, even when an active crime scene overtook her nonexistent Christmas plans. The excavation freed her from the holiday hustle and bustle she detested more than the insufferable game and parks officer reigning as security over the site.

He'd gone, for now, but if his previous behavior was any indicator, there'd soon be more rounds in futility. Those who misjudged Taya's petite five-foot, ninety-pound stature for weakness learned the hard way that her stubbornness came packaged like dynamite and equaled her determination.

Dr. Taya McGill would never again succumb to a uniformed bully.

"It's just you and me, friend. You're safe to share your secrets," Taya said, brushing back dirt from the exposed skull. Her coworkers mocked the unconventional method of talking aloud to the victim, but the process worked for her. And since she spent the majority of her time alone, who did it bother, anyway?

Unpredictable weather had hindered the recovery of the human remains, hindering the dig's progression. The frigid winter temperatures had banked at a high—if that was a relative term—of negative four degrees. The radical increasing wind speeds over the past hour had further complicated things. No overhead streetlamps illuminated the onyx sky. Rolling hills and the occasional farm nestled in an endless snow-covered landscape surrounded over three hundred acres of Ashfall Fossil Beds State Park in the northeastern corner of Royal, Nebraska.

She shivered and tugged the zipper of her down-alternative parka as high as it would go, tucking her nose in the warmth. It was after midnight, but Taya's ongoing battle with insomnia provided her the excuse to continue working. The victim buried in the shallow grave deserved justice. As did those mourning her.

Taya leaned down and paused with her brush midair. She'd already exposed most of the skeletal form and prepared to collect the remains for transport to her laboratory at the University of Nebraska in Lincoln. Something red near the thoracic vertebrae peeked through the earth. With a delicate swipe, she uncovered the object. A small deflated latex balloon.

Taya sighed. The find wasn't unusual. Addicts ingested the balloons as a method of muling illegal drugs. Was that this victim's story?

She reached for her camera, documenting the new discovery. Using her gloved fingertips, she lifted and inspected the balloon under the powerful multidimensional LED tripod work light. A bulbous exterior was common, but this item was flat, concealing something hard inside. Curiosity building, Taya removed a pair of scissors from her bag. She sliced through the latex, releasing a SIM card, similar to the type she used in her digital camera.

Excitement building, Taya again documented the evidence, then swapped the cards, watching as the first of two videos came to life. The footage appeared to be shot from a vehicle's dashboard cam. An attractive thirtysomething woman sat in the driver's seat. Heavy makeup accentuated by thick black eyeliner emphasized her large hazel eyes. She brushed a dark curl from her face and the light glimmered off her ring.

Taya instantly recognized the delicate silver piece as one she'd recovered on the body's left hand earlier that evening. Comprised of two merging bands, the first section of silver swept upward where two opposing diamond butterflies sat at the center. Either the killer hadn't seen the ring or hadn't thought to remove it before burying the victim.

The woman spoke into the camera. "This is DEA Agent Patrice Nunes. Today is September 3 and I'm preparing for Brando's arrival. If everything goes as planned, I will have the proof to expose him and take down his operation." Her brows furrowed, and she glanced to the side. Her question was barely audible: "Why—"

Taya brought the device closer, eyes glued to the screen as both passenger-side doors opened. Two men entered the car simultaneously, one in the front seat, the second in the back.

"Brando ain't comin,' Butterfly," the man in the front seat said. An asymmetrical tattoo of the skeletal facial structure covered the left side of his face.

Taya gasped at his shocking appearance, but her apprehension transformed into criticism at the disproportionate and inaccurately placed jawbone inked on his skin.

"Skull, who's your friend?" Patrice asked. Though she wore an indifferent expression, her voice hitched up a notch.

He leaned back with a serpentine grin that made Taya shudder. "Meet my new partner, Raptor."

By comparison, Raptor, the handsome man centered in the rear seat, filled the space with his large frame and muscular build. Dark thick hair, cut short, framed his rugged unshaven face. He angled closer and his stormy gray eyes flitted to the camera, hesitating before he averted his gaze.

Almost as if he saw Taya watching. Her pulse increased with anticipation. She glanced down at the human remains. "Are you Patrice?" Had one or both of the men killed and buried her here?

The woman's voice directed Taya's attention back to the video.

"If you're hoping to score ice, I don't have it on me. Give me the cash and I'll drop it off later." Patrice returned to a casual pose; her tone almost bored.

Ice? Was she referencing the street name for methamphetamines?

A fresh gust of wind whipped Taya's long blond hair across her face, blinding her, and an ear-piercing howl had her jumping to her feet. She tripped on the tarp used to cover the exposed space and stumbled back, knocking over the tripod light. In an effort to reset the base, she lost her grip on the camera and it tumbled to the ground.

Frustrated, Taya swiped away the wild tendrils and tucked them behind her ears. The collapsed LED lamp lay on its side, casting shadows over the grave.

Thick darkness pressed in around her, but she forced herself to remain still, listening. Had she imagined the howl? Coyotes prowled this area.

Her heart pounded so hard it consumed her senses, but she refused to surrender to fear.

Several long seconds passed without another sound and her apprehension turned to embarrassment. Thankfully, there weren't witnesses.

Taya righted the lamp and recovered her camera. She removed the SIM card—determined to watch the rest of the videos from the comfort of her Winnebago parked three hundred feet away—and reached for an empty evidence bag.

Her frustration increased at the realization that she'd forgotten to replenish the supply. She slid the card into her coat pocket, intending to log it later.

Uneasiness crept between her shoulder blades. Yellow crime scene tape cordoned off the work space, snapping against the increasing wind. She scanned the area again, then heaved a long sigh, conceding that it was time to close up for the night.

Movement in her peripheral vision stilled her.

Taya lifted the tripod lamp. "Who's there?"

Silence responded, but she couldn't shake the lingering sensation someone was watching her.

Stop it, Taya. She hoisted her excavation tool bag onto her shoulder, then tugged the tarp over the grave, and secured the edges to the fixed anchors. *Now, turn off the lamp and walk.* Only half of the distance to where her prized possession—a used Minnie Winnie—sat parked at the top of the hill beside the Rhino Barn. The tall metal pole barn housed fossils still embedded in ash.

Just another exercise in overcoming her fear of the dark. And she would succeed.

One terrifying moment at a time.

Taya hesitated, then exhaled a fortifying breath and a reassuring scripture. "I can do all things through Christ which strengtheneth me." With a final perusal, she flipped off the tripod and absorbed the adrenaline coursing through her. She wrapped her fingers around the bag's strap and started out on shaking legs.

Again, movement in her peripheral.

Taya spun but spotted nothing. Abandoning her attempted self-soothing therapy plan, she bolted full speed.

Her feet pounded against the frozen ground, and her breath came in rapid, panting bursts. The weight of her bag beat against her hip.

Almost there.

And then she saw them: tall forms leaning against the Rhino Barn obscured by the shadows. The first shifted into the light and crossed his arms over his chest.

She slowed, recognizing them both from the video she'd watched only minutes before. Skull. The skeleton-tattooed man.

His partner moved closer. Raptor.

Taya increased her pace to a full sprint, reaching the Winnebago, and lunged inside. She pulled the door shut, gripping the knob, lungs heaving with exertion and cold. Her fingers danced in a frenzied rhythm as she tried to secure the lock.

At last, the bolt clicked into place.

One man barreled into the thin metal barrier, jolting her. Taya screamed and stepped up into the motor home scouring the space for a weapon, then flipped off the interior light, hoping they wouldn't see her.

In a haphazard motion, she dropped her bag onto the cluttered dinette, knocking her laptop to the floor. Taya reached into the kitchen drawer and grasped a knife.

Another ram against the small RV, followed by the macabre chant of, "Little pig, little pig, let me in."

She spun, searching for her cell phone and spotted the device on the nightstand beside her bed. Still charging. Beneath the large window.

She moved closer to the sleeping quarters.

The beating on the door grew more intense, bending the edges inward. He'd tear it down for sure.

Just one final step to her phone.

The ramming stopped.

No more taunting.

Had they gone? She froze in place her gaze bouncing between the door and the window.

The same cry she'd heard earlier echoed outside. A coyote? Had the animal scared off the intruders?

She rushed around the bed and snagged her phone, yanking it from the wall.

A strange tap emanated behind her and the window shattered. Thick arms wrapped around her waist, tugging her toward the opening.

Taya fought, kicking and swinging, inadvertently dropping her phone and sliced the knife through the air. She hit something. The intruder jerked her sideways, slamming her into the window frame and knocked the knife out of her hand. She clawed and braced her legs against the wall to keep him from pulling her out the window. In her last extreme effort, Taya bit his arm.

It worked.

He yelled, releasing her.

She lunged over the bed toward the doorway, but was halted by a blast of cold air.

Skull stepped inside and flipped on the light. He sported that same sinister grin she'd seen in Patrice's video, and a large pistol. His blackened eyelid gave the illusion of an optical cavity and the ginger goatee betrayed his bald head's attempt at disguising his hair color.

She glanced over her shoulder, cornered. Frosty wind whipped through the broken window.

No place to run.

"Who are you?" she gasped, aware of the answer as she studied the familiar skeleton-tattooed face. Her gaze traveled to the gun. Science she understood. Anatomy she understood. Weapons not so much. "What do you want? Money? Drugs?"

"Just you, darlin'," Skull answered. "Ooh wee. Brando

didn't say you were a looker." He released a guttural growl, twisting her stomach into a knot.

She did a partial pivot, spotting Raptor climbing in through the broken window.

"Does she have the goods?" Raptor asked in a voice so deep it rumbled.

Skull laughed. "Nah, man, she *is* the goods. We're gonna eliminate the good doctor here."

Disbelief at the two intruders had her blinking several times, her mind replaying their part in Patrice's video.

Taya leaped, landing on the dinette, then jumped to the small sofa.

The men advanced from their positions opposite her. Blocking any escape.

Skull grasped her hair and yanked her off the cushion.

Taya cringed against his relentless hold. "Whatever you want, just take it." She squeezed her eyes shut, expecting the worst.

She focused on each thrash of the motor home's flapping door as it slammed into the wall. Beaten into submission by the erratic whims of the gusty wind. Evidence of a struggle.

She would die today. *Lord, help me.*

Skull released a grunted *oomph*, and the pressure on her head ceased.

Taya startled, eyes open, and glanced down at her assailant. He lay sprawled out, unconscious at her feet. She screamed, then covered her mouth and staggered into the back of the driver's seat.

Raptor stepped forward, hand outstretched. "I know you're scared, but Skull won't be out for long. I'll help you, but we have to get out of here. Now!"

Confusion and terror froze her in place while she skimmed the area for a weapon. Her surveillance stopped on the silver ring encased in the evidence bag on the dinette. Why hadn't she put it away?

Raptor followed her gaze and his eyes widened as if he recognized the item.

The rumble of an engine interrupted their silent standoff. He peered out the small window above the sink. "Someone's coming," he relayed as if she couldn't hear the approaching truck.

A new appreciation for the obnoxious game and parks officer washed over her. If only she could get his attention.

With his back to her, Taya reached for the ring, accidentally brushing it off the table in her clumsy attempt. It landed on the bench across from her. Out of reach. *No.*

"We have to leave. Now." He grabbed her arm. His touch was strong, but not abrasive.

Taya straightened to her full height, shoulders stiff. "I'm not going anywhere with you. However, that vehicle belongs to an officer. Turn yourself in or run away. I won't report you as recompense for protecting me from your friend." She gestured at Skull still splayed at her feet.

"Dr. McGill, you can come with me voluntarily or I will be forced to drag you out of here."

"How do you know my name?" She inched closer to the door slamming against the wall with the wind.

Skull groaned, and she looked down. In one stride, Raptor bound the man's wrists with thin plastic straps then glanced up at her, a storm brewing in his eyes. "If we don't leave now, we'll be dead by morning."

Alcohol, Tobacco and Firearms Agent Keegan Stryker fought the urge to throw Dr. McGill over his shoulder and run from the motor home. The danger they faced increased a hundredfold with every passing second.

"Raptor, is it?"

He jerked at her familiar use of his alias. Was she involved with the traffickers? Her next words nixed that concern.

"I refuse to go anywhere with you. Get out of my home."

The petite attractive blonde was no threat, though her stance conveyed she intended to fight.

Keegan's patience evaporated, but he didn't dare speak the truth with the possibility that Skull might overhear. He motioned to the door and placed a finger against his lips. "Please."

"Fine," she mumbled, sidestepping Skull.

Keegan allowed her to exit first, then trailed close behind. With a final glance over his shoulder confirming Skull was still out, he closed the dented door.

Dr. McGill paused, her attention on the approaching headlights bouncing over the ridge and drawing closer. Ashfall State Historical Park Recreation Road curved at the bottom of the park entrance from 517th Avenue. The distance and geography provided temporary cover, but the driver would spot them once he crested the hill.

Keegan anticipated her foolish move. *Don't do it.* "We need—"

McGill bolted for the road, arms flailing and screeching at the top of her lungs, cutting off Keegan's words.

Jaw tight, he sprinted after her and snagged her around the waist. In a fluid motion, he hefted her slight build onto his shoulder in a fireman carry. The positioning made it difficult for her to continue bellowing, though she beat on his back with the force of a tiny ball-peen hammer.

"Put me down, you beast!"

Keegan ignored her, fixated on getting as far from Skull as possible before the man came to and realized they'd gone. With the Winnebago blocking them, he prayed the newcomer hadn't seen McGill's frenzied efforts.

The engine of the pickup she'd advised as belonging to a game and park's officer grew louder. Keegan descended the hill to Skull's beater parked in the valley below. Mc-Gill wriggled and shrieked in a vain effort at deterring his pace. *Please, Lord, let the officer arrest Skull and buy me time to get Dr. McGill to safety.*

At last, they reached the car and Keegan set her down.

She huffed and staggered back, hands fisted at her sides. Even with the dark of night shadowing her facial features, he was certain she was hornet-furious. And cute, too. "How dare you!"

"I'm sorry, Dr. McGill, but you're in danger." Keegan rubbed his face and forced a calm he didn't feel into his tone. "I realize this sounds nuts to you, and I promise to explain. In the car. We have to get out of here. If Skull wakes up and finds us missing, you and I are both dead!" And everything he'd done over the last thirteen months would be in vain.

"How do you know my name? I'm not going anywhere with you," she contended, planting her hands on her hips. The actions didn't disguise the tremor in her voice.

He sighed. "Would you rather ride in the trunk?"

She paused and blinked twice. With a glance at the beater, she opened her mouth, then shut it again.

Keegan inhaled, contemplating how much to share with her. Now that they were out of reach of Skull's hearing, he settled on the basics. "You called me Raptor. That's my alias. My real name is Keegan Stryker. I'm an ATF agent working deep undercover."

She shook her head. "As in Alcohol, Tobacco and Firearms? What on earth does that have to do with me? How were you aware I'd be at Ashfall this evening? Why not arrest the man that tried to kill me?"

The woman rapid-fired her questions faster than he could respond. He waited for her to suck in a breath and said, "We don't have time for this little clash of wills. Get in the car." Keegan tugged open the passenger door.

"No." She shoved her hand in her coat pocket and her

eyes widened. She turned to look at the hill behind them and repeated, "No."

What was she searching for?

"Now."

McGill pinched her lips together, then exhaled with exaggerated vehemence and slid into the passenger seat.

Keegan shut the door and raced to the driver's side. He started the engine—grateful Skull always kept the keys in the ignition for a fast getaway—and sped across the prairie. His thoughts bounced around like the tires against the uneven terrain.

"Turn on your headlights! Are you trying to kill us?"

He glanced over at McGill, her hand clutching the door's handle. "We can't chance it." The limited light also prevented him from seeing the road, but that beat the alternative.

"I did as you ordered. Now explain why an undercover ATF agent just kidnapped me."

"I don't want to endanger you any more than necessary. Less information is better."

"Absolutely unacceptable! You will tell me what's going on and take me to the police!"

Keegan bit his cheek. "If we go to the local PD, it'll blow my cover. You'll be safe with my team."

"Is that why you refused to wait for Officer Folze?"

"Who?"

"The game and parks officer who would've helped us until you threw me over your shoulder in that barbaric manner."

McGill talked too much, and he needed quiet to think.

"Your insufficient response fails to address my concerns. Why did you and that skeleton-looking man burst into my motor home?"

Keegan concentrated on the blurring yellow lines and snow-bordered road. "Skull said we were going on a new job tonight. I assumed he meant a run to meet suppliers."

"Suppliers for what?"

"Weapons trafficking."

She gasped. "How can such corrupt activities happen at Ashfall? It's a park. A closed park at that. Far removed from the city."

If she only comprehended the crime hidden in the countryside. "Again, let's err on the side of caution and minimal details."

She harrumphed. "Your friend Skull seemed intent on 'eliminating' me, as he so eloquently advised back there. You nearly dragged me through a window! Do I appear naive enough to presume you're an innocent bystander?"

"No, ma'am, I had no clue the goal was to kill you tonight. Sorry about the window. For the record, that would've worked until you almost stabbed me. And thanks for biting me, too." Years of training taught Keegan to act fast and process later. He'd knocked Skull out with an occipital stun to his thick, empty head. The reminder brought on a new rendition of throbbing pain from the impact.

Her posture remained stiff. "What motive would anyone, especially that Skull animal, have to kill me?"

"I was hoping you'd answer that question for me." He gripped the steering wheel's worn ripped cover where the torn laces exposed the underlying plastic.

"I have no enemies. I live alone. I'm not wealthy."

She was single. Not that it mattered, but something about the statement appealed to him. Keegan shook his head, forcing the thought away. There was a connection between Dr. McGill and the traffickers. Once he established that, he'd have a better handle on the situation. "Are you familiar with a man named Brando?"

She hesitated, and he glanced over, but she averted her eyes, facing her window. "I've met no one by that name."

Her response raised a red flag. What was she hiding? "Are you involved in dealing drugs?"

He didn't look in her direction but felt the blast of her death glare. "Are you out of your mind? Of course not!" The indignation in her voice didn't surprise him. "And before you ask, I don't own a gun or any other firearms."

Doubtful she was a supplier to Brando. So why did he want her dead? "I need to contact my CO and get you somewhere safe."

"CO?"

"Commanding officer." They'd have to hide out at his safe house in the village of Verdigre, unknown to Brando and Skull. However, driving there in Skull's car wasn't an option. The old beater didn't have GPS tracking, but Keegan couldn't risk it. "First, we need a new ride."

"That's an understatement," she said, her small frame melting into the aged seat cushions. "I'm surprised this contraption moves."

Masquerading as a weapons trafficker required living with criminals and eliminated his expectations of nice things. Brando's men bragged about their lengthy rap sheets and many included prison terms. None had money or possessions and almost all were drug-addicted, making them indebted to Brando. The vile taskmaster relished the power of his mysterious identity, and Keegan was impatient to dethrone him.

"I demand you take me to the police."

She'd never understand his reservations about avoiding the local sheriff's department. "You'll be safe with my team."

"This is absurd. By what stretch of your neurotic and overactive imagination would you think I'd be naive enough to believe this?"

Keegan shot a glance in her direction. "Your enemies are deadly, and they're coming for you whether or not you believe in them."

TWO

Keegan parked in front of the rundown barn doubling as his off-site secret garage. He hated providing Dr. McGill with unnecessary knowledge of his hiding place, but there wasn't time to play coy. "Stay here. We've got to trade vehicles."

Taya scooted to the edge of her seat. "Agent Stryker, a simultaneous switch would be more prudent and efficient, don't you agree?"

He studied her. In a word, yes. Except he didn't trust her not to drive off.

She tilted her head and a blond tendril swept over her shoulder. "You needn't worry I'll run away."

Great. He had to work on his facial expressions if they'd betrayed him that easily. "Yeah, okay."

He exited the driver's seat while she rounded the front of the car, then slid behind the wheel.

Keegan rushed into the building and aimed for the hay bale at the far side, removing his SUV keys from between the blocks. He returned to the vehicle and pulled out of the garage, prepared to speed after Skull's jalopy. To his relief, McGill drove into the vacated space and shut off the engine. She exited the car, entered the SUV's passenger seat, and passed him the keys.

"Thanks for remembering these." He pocketed the keys.

She gave a slight jerk of her head and snapped her seat belt.

Even if Skull found this place, which was doubtful, he wouldn't have an easy time getting the beater to run. Although knowing the criminal's history, hot-wiring a car wasn't inconceivable. Especially one as old as this.

"Give me a second to lock up." Keegan completed the final touches by cutting the car's fuel line. Satisfied the hindrance would detain Skull, he closed the barn doors and returned to the driver's seat.

McGill removed something from her coat pocket and held it out to him. "Gum?"

"No, thanks."

She withdrew a piece and popped it into her mouth. The blowing air vents wafted a sweet minty scent. "Where are you taking me?"

Keegan stole a peek in her direction, but the dim lights provided little illumination. "To my safe house in Verdigre."

The rhythmic snapping of her gum replaced the inquisitive Dr. McGill's interrogations. An aggravation that had Keegan preferring her incessant questions.

The otherwise quiet commute allowed him time to process the evening's events and his shoulders tightened. He'd recognized his stepsister Patrice's butterfly ring the moment he'd laid eyes on it. How had the anthropologist gotten a hold of it? "Dr. McGill—"

"Taya, please. I'm not preoccupied with titles."

A beautiful name that fit her well. "I saw a woman's ring on your table. Where did you get it?"

"On a fourth phalange," she answered.

Keegan shot her a look. She might not care about labels, but she flaunted her intelligence. He'd placate her need for superiority. "I'm an ATF agent, not a doctor. Could you relay that in layman's terms?"

"Finger bone, right hand," she said triumphantly, popping her gum several times. A habit, he noted, she did often. Too often.

Dread tanked his stomach. After the death of Patrice's father, her mother, Ione, commissioned the custom piece as a memorial keepsake. Patrice never removed the ring from her finger.

Guilt propelled his fear and taunted him. *She's dead.*

And Keegan was the reason.

The memories of his last encounter with his stepsister danced before him. He'd never seen Patrice as excited as the day she asked his advice regarding her new career opportunity working undercover for the DEA. Ever the supportive brother, he'd encouraged her to climb the ladder of success. Never considering the selfishness of his words.

Too busy with his own ambition, he'd gone undercover soon thereafter and infiltrated the trafficking cartel. He and Patrice hadn't communicated again until their paths crossed inadvertently in their respective roles. Keegan had fought to disguise his surprise when he spotted her working the drug connection in the same cartel. Unable to communicate for fear of blowing their cover, too much time had passed before he'd become aware she'd gone missing.

Keegan gripped the steering wheel, grounding himself. His CO, Otto Hawkins, had broken the news to him. The supposed indisputable evidence confirmed Patrice had deserted the DEA and made off with a significant amount of money and drugs. The idiotic move planted her as an enemy to both the criminals and law enforcement. It was no wonder she'd disappeared.

Keegan refused to believe the accusations, however, he couldn't deny drug use and gang involvement had been present in Patrice's teen years. Her history permitted a tiny seed of doubt to plant in his heart. Surely, she wouldn't have returned to that life. Not after all she'd achieved as a DEA agent.

He shoved down the painful memories, returning to the comfort and familiarity of his investigative process. Perhaps Patrice wasn't dead. Perhaps she'd sold the ring? Or someone had stolen it and that person was wearing the ring Taya had found. He redirected his attention to her. "What brought you to Ashfall?"

She lifted her chin. "As usual, law enforcement's communication continues to fail between agencies. I'm a forensic anthropologist, summoned here to excavate human remains found at the prehistoric park."

"How do you know they're not old bones belonging to a cave person?"

She sighed as if irked, and her tone dangled one notch above condescending. "Agent Stryker—"

"Keegan. I'm not hung up on titles, either."

That brought a grin to her full lips. "Fine. Keegan, human bones would postdate the fossils. They simply do not belong there."

"Then how did you know there were bones at Ashfall?"

"An off-leash canine wandered into the park and returned to his owners carrying a femur."

Keegan processed the term. "Femur. As in a leg bone?"

"Yes. My team and I used ground-penetrating radar to locate the burial site."

Was Patrice buried in the grave? He could barely speak the next words over the foreboding clogging his throat. "Have you identified the person?"

Taya sat back in the seat, crossing her arms over her chest. "No, but the skull has a rounded forehead sharpened around the top of the upper eye rim. Distinct characteristics confirming she is a Caucasian adult female. I estimate in her thirties at the time of death. I'll know more after I perform a thorough examination to determine actual height and age."

Something told Keegan the good doctor would confirm the body as thirty-three-year-old Patrice Nunes. His stomach wrenched.

His stepsister was lying in that grave.

Guilt returned and Keegan drank its bitterness.

He'd failed Patrice. The emotions reaffirmed his dedication to finish the mission and expose Brando. Maybe his stepsister was still alive, and he'd find her. Either way, the victim buried at Ashfall deserved justice. Keegan would arrest the murderer. It was what he did best. "Have you notified anyone of your findings?"

"Agent, you kidnapped me from my motor home before I had a chance to do anything."

Something in her comment conveyed deceit. What was she hiding?

Consistent in her approach, Taya inquired, "If you're an ATF agent, why didn't you arrest the people you were after? Starting with Skull?"

"It's complicated."

She snorted. "Is that an arrogant cop-ism at thwarting my questions?"

Definitely, because Taya had no idea what she asked. The things he'd seen and done to maintain his cover had him delving deeper into the trafficking world than he cared to admit.

She'd never understand what he'd lost.

And what they'd stolen.

Focus, Stryker. If the body was Patrice, Keegan had a whole new motivation for identifying Brando and solving this case.

He would not permit a murderer to go free.

Scratch that. This was personal. He wouldn't allow his sister's killer to go free. "Have you determined the cause of death?" He couldn't bear to say Patrice's name. Not saying it made her death less real, but his gut argued the body was her.

Taya stopped snapping her gum for a moment. "COD is undetermined as of yet. I must continue to ask, moreover, what connection is there between these criminals and me?"

Exactly. "Were there any other clues in the grave?"

Taya paused a moment too long.

"Is there anything you haven't told me?" he probed.

"Keegan," she said his name as if it bored her, "I have answered your questions. Considering you're withholding information from me, for my safety, as you've explained, do not push me to tell you things you're not privy to, either."

Touché. But still avoidance. Definitely hiding something.

Taya redirected. "Do you think they're trying to prevent me from identifying the body?"

"If you haven't finished the excavation or shared your findings, that would be my assumption." Concern regarding the site's protection had him contemplating their return to Ashfall. "Are cameras providing surveillance over the scene?"

"Officer Folze has designation of security at Ashfall. Another reason we should've contacted him rather than running away."

Keegan ignored the slam. As long as there was protective detail over the site, he had time to hide Taya.

Who killed Patrice and why? Did one of the traffickers discover her real identity? Was someone on the inside involved? With the DEA and ATF working together, he couldn't be sure of every person with knowledge of the mission. And if an insider had silenced Patrice, who could he trust?

Keegan sighed. "The man ordering your elimination will

not stop until you're dead. And if he believes I've turned on the group, I'll be next."

"So, tell me, Agent Stryker, what's your plan? If he is all-powerful and relentless, what am I to do? Remain in hiding my entire life?"

"Nope. Just until I finish this case."

"And do share. What's your time estimation?"

Keegan worked his jaw. "As long as it takes."

"That's absolutely unacceptable. I have a job to do, and I will not be deemed incompetent or a weakling who flees from her assignment. Find another way."

An interesting statement that revealed a tiny glimpse into the intelligent woman's reasoning. She was obviously dedicated to her work, and her bravery was commendable. Keegan glanced at her. "Do you understand what I'm saying to you? These men will kill you. Why do they want you dead? If it's because you can identify the body, we need access to the site."

"Well, we certainly cannot do anything outside of Ashfall."

"Yes, Dr. McGill, I'm aware of that. However, your safety is my first priority." Keegan's undercover world had allowed him a lot of personal discretion without explanation. He wasn't used to detailing out his processes or thoughts.

"I believe the most prudent course of action is to return to Ashfall," she went on, "with police protection allowing me to accomplish the complete excavation."

Keegan shook his head. If the victim was Patrice, knowing her identity wasn't sufficient. He had to know what had happened and who was responsible. "I agree. But we can't return. Not yet."

"What do you propose? Your criminal connections aren't naive enough to believe I was frightened away in the middle of the night."

Keegan studied her. She was right, Brando wouldn't stop until he'd finished the job Skull failed to complete. He had to make sure Brando didn't try again. An idea beamed. "You're correct. Hiding you isn't enough."

She jutted out her chin. "Finally. I'm glad you're a reasonable man."

"The only one way to stop Brando is to prove to him you're already dead and unable to identify the remains."

Her big blue eyes widened. "I don't understand."

"We'll fake your death and give Brando what he wants. A dead anthropologist."

Taya sat at Keegan's two-person dinette wearing her perfected mask of confidence and surveyed the bland microscopic living room. A single sofa, end table and lamp occupied the space. No TV, personal effects or holiday trinkets.

The safe house—though she had serious doubts whether this ramshackle structure qualified—sat shielded from the main road in the middle of a rural area. Nondescript and hidden beneath a canopy of overgrown trees and brush, the place was nearly invisible. If she screamed at the top of her lungs, no one would hear her cries for help. So, if Keegan wasn't who he claimed to be—though he'd shown her his ATF identification badge—she was a dead woman. Although based on his ludicrous scheme, that was inevitable.

Hands folded to stop them from shaking, Taya didn't dare speak, fearful her voice would betray her in a weak quiver. She never lacked for words; in fact, they bombarded her brain in an endless playlist. Not that she was a big talker, but she knew when to talk and when to remain quiet. One of her best attributes, at least according to her mother.

However, it was foreboding in every conceivable possibility that prevented her from speaking.

The long drive to his safe house gave her plenty of time

to think, pray and stress. Not necessarily in that order. Regret at not speeding off when they'd exchanged vehicles added to her frustration. Though she'd been focused on getting away from Skull.

Keegan hadn't tried to harm her, but she remained unconvinced of his altruistic motives to save her. And as much as she detested law enforcement, she'd be better off in their care than his. All her contemplations funneled toward a single priority.

Escape.

If only she had a way to call for help. She pictured her cell phone lying somewhere on the floor of her motor home.

Keegan refused to listen to reason, stubbornly determined to follow through with his ridiculous plan. He'd paced the same pattern for so long, she worried he'd wear a path right through the wooden floorboards.

A shudder rumbled through her body at the memory of Skull. Evading him had been crucial, but she didn't have to hang around here and hide. If Keegan was really working undercover—and she wasn't convinced of that—was it his duty to protect her? And how long would he stand guard?

Taya couldn't shake the lingering doubt. If experience taught her anything, it was that law enforcement could unknowingly hire great actors and fantastic liars.

Just like Jeremy, her FBI agent ex-fiancé, and his current wife, also an FBI agent, Gail. The mere thought of them sent a new wave of irritation through Taya. She trusted very few humans, none of whom included law enforcement. After all, she'd known Jeremy seven years. Supported him through college and his training at the FBI Academy. He'd promised her a future together as soon as he graduated.

Squelching her own dreams, she'd turned down the golden opportunity to be a forensic anthropologist for the FBI. Jeremy had discouraged her, stating the litany of downfalls in a couple working for the same organization.

Against her better judgment, she'd surrendered to his request and declined the employment offer, promising to follow Jeremy wherever his career sent them.

In the ultimate betrayal, right before graduation, Jeremy announced he'd fallen in love with another FBI recruit. They'd run off into the sunset, shattering Taya's heart, and she'd curled up in Nebraska, burying her pathetic dreams.

If the government couldn't spot a good liar, how could she trust any agent they produced?

Taya returned to her current situation. Keegan had bolted the doors, one at the front of the house, another at the back. He'd parked the SUV in the attached garage, and opening the large door would be noisy. And if she recalled correctly, the keys were tucked out of reach in his jeans pocket.

Fine. Plan B. Fake contentment while hiding out with Keegan until she escaped. She'd go to the police, report Skull and demand security protection to complete her job at Ashfall.

Taya assessed Keegan's pacing form. The one thing she couldn't deny was the man's magnetic draw and handsome exterior. Keegan Stryker, if that was his real name, was tall, broad shouldered and comprised of solid muscle. His dark jeans and black motorcycle boots gave him a dangerous air, combined with his deep voice. Taya would never admit it to him, but she enjoyed when he spoke. His presence commanded attention. He'd been terse, yet his mannerisms never segued into rudeness.

As much as she wanted to trust him, if he was an ATF agent, he fell into the law enforcement category, meaning he *could* have the propensity to lie. He'd take care of Number One and leave her to suffer the aftermath.

She resumed chomping on her peppermint gum, coagulating it into a rubbery mass. Still, it helped calm her nerves. "Are you reconsidering your plan?" she blurted, releasing the doubt that had traversed through her mind a million different ways. She hoped her words registered in her rescuer's brain.

Keegan appeared undaunted. "Nope. I'm figuring out the details."

"We've been here for hours." She groaned and leaned back in the chair. Intellectualism meant Taya appreciated careful preparation and consideration, but even her contemplations hadn't lasted this long. "How about brainstorming together?"

"No, thanks."

"Of course, I forget law enforcement officers have the market on brainstorming plans."

He frowned. "I didn't mean to offend you. I appreciate your offer, but I've got it. We need photographic evidence of your death so we'll fake a gunshot wound. That's the easiest. Thing is, there's only one chance to pull this off."

She swallowed the lump in her throat. He made it sound so simple. "Why haven't you contacted your CO?"

He paused. "I'm not sure it's safe."

Aha. Proof he was a liar. "You said we'd hide here until your CO came to get me. Now you're saying otherwise. Make up your mind, Agent."

"I beg your pardon?" He worked his jaw, and narrowed his gray eyes.

Taya refused to look away, though it was clear she'd angered him.

They held their silent standoff for several seconds before Keegan replied, "Dr. McGill, I realize I'm asking a lot for you to trust me at this point. Let me assure you, when I'm able to share more, I will." He turned on his heel, dismissing her.

What if his death ruse was a lie, too? Perhaps there was a window in the bathroom. She'd climb out and run for help. Taya shoved back her chair and stood.

Keegan spun to face her. "Where are you going?"

"Are you holding me hostage?"

"No."

"I must use your restroom. Do you need to accompany me there also?"

If she wasn't mistaken, the man's handsome face flushed a shade of pink. Had she embarrassed him? He pointed a muscular arm to the door in the center of the hallway.

Without comment, she stomped to the room. Her disappointment was immediate. No window, only a stand-up shower, toilet and pedestal sink.

Fantastic. She leaned against the wall and grimaced at her reflection. With a few finger-combs, she tamed the wild wisps of blond hair framing her round face, but nothing besides sleep would relieve her bloodshot eyes. Resigned with her efforts to clean up her appearance, she tugged open the door and returned to her seat at the table.

Keegan dropped onto the chair opposite her. "We'll take the pictures outside. Lesser light works to our advantage."

"If you say so."

"Let's do this." He pushed back his chair, removed a gun from his waistband and set it down. He withdrew bottles of ketchup and chocolate syrup from the refrigerator and combined the contents in a bowl.

"I assume you're making fake blood?" she asked, realizing her tone sounded snarky.

"Yep."

Taya forced her voice to steady. "How do you propose to shoot me without shooting me?"

"All we need is picture proof." Keegan walked to the bedroom and emerged carrying a yellow T-shirt. "Change into this and give me your hoodie."

She glanced down at her favorite purple hoodie before taking the ugly proffered shirt from his outstretched hand. Without a word, she moved to the bathroom and changed, then returned to the living room. "Okay, now what?" She handed him the clothing.

Keegan smeared the blood-like concoction on the material covering her heart. "Stay here. I'll be right back."

She started to protest, then realized it was pointless. With a shrug, Taya dropped onto the sofa. She flinched at the blast of gunfire, grateful he'd not witnessed her weakness.

Keegan returned, carrying her now bullet-riddled clothing. "Put this on."

Taya walked to the bathroom for the third time and pulled it on. She wrinkled her nose at the strong smell of gunpowder and sighed at the ruined hoodie.

She stepped out and met his satisfied grin. "And what happens when they want to see the body?"

"I'll convince them I tossed you into the Niobrara River."

"Seems you've thought of everything."

"Let's hope so."

He led her outside to a wooded area behind the house. "Lie down on the ground and keep your eyes open. Stare upward and don't blink or move."

"If you say so."

"The pictures just have to look authentic enough for Brando to believe you're dead. Then we'll work on getting you to safety."

Taya lowered herself to the snow-covered ground facing the darkened sky. "Say when."

"When!" A deep chuckle followed the command—most assuredly not Keegan's—jerking Taya upright.

No. Oh, please. No. Staring in disbelief, Taya scooted to her feet on shaky legs. Terror swooped over her like a bloodthirsty bat and sent her pulse raging.

Skull stood across from them. Gun aimed. "What's up, Raptor? I see you have our friend. But there's no need to play dead, Dr. McGill. I'll finish the job this time."

THREE

Keegan's blood froze at Skull's threat. He stood stone still while his mind raced out of control.

How had Skull found the safe house? Worse, how much had he overheard?

Keegan's focus steadied on Taya, mentally willing her to remain calm. "Dude, it's about time you showed up."

The words had Taya's beautiful blue eyes bulging, and her hands flew to her throat. Her gaze bounced from Keegan to Skull in a silent plea of desperation. He gave a slight jerk of his head, then slowly lowered his arm, palm up, signaling Taya not to move. Hand grazing his hip—absent of his nine millimeter—Keegan remembered his weapon sat on the dining table and his stomach tanked. He'd grown too comfortable here. How had he been so stupid as to leave it behind?

In a single motion, Keegan pivoted and avoided Taya's eyes. "Kudos on escaping the game and parks officer." He prayed Taya understood his subterfuge.

Skull's lips flattened beneath his murderous narrowed glare, grip tight on his favorite 1911 Colt. The barrel aimed at Keegan grew to canon-size proportions. If Taya ran, Skull would shoot her. Keegan had to get closer and disarm Skull while keeping her in his line of sight. Keegan shifted slightly, allowing himself a better visual over both parties.

"Never pegged you for a backstabber." Skull's stare drove an icy knife into Keegan's chest that had nothing to do with the negative temperatures.

"Dude, you know me." Keegan inserted himself in the space between Taya and Skull. A human shield to protect her.

"You betrayed me." Skull's whiny accusation contrasted with his malicious persona.

"Put that gun down before you hurt yourself." Keegan gestured at the 1911. "Quit talking crazy. It's too cold. Let's go inside." He took a step toward the house.

"You're a coward and traitor." Skull lifted the gun higher. "Funny thing, Raptor. Last I remember, you were standin' behind me. Then I wake up on the floor of the motor home. How do you reckon that happened?"

Keegan shook his head. "You need to lay off the ice, it's starting to affect your memory. We were about to kill her when the G and P cop showed up."

Why hadn't Skull mentioned his wrists bound with zip ties? How had he broken them off? Had the game and parks officer even seen Skull?

A frown deepened Skull's ugly face. "There weren't no cop. Just you, me and the doctor."

"There most certainly was," Taya interrupted from behind Keegan. "Officer Gunner Folze. He drove up right after you trespassed into my home."

Skull glared at her, his jaw tight. "Nobody asked you."

Keegan redirected his attention. "See? Man, I couldn't carry you and her. I kidnapped her and blazed outta there. Been waiting to hear from you ever since."

Skull seemed to mull over the details, processing them in his empty brain. Keegan pushed on. "Now that you're here, we'll finish the job."

"Nah, looks to me like you had other ideas." Skull turned his pistol sideways in the manner common to gang members. Though intimidating, the ineffective angle provided a less accurate shot. No need to provide that helpful note.

Keegan struggled for something to divert Skull. "So whatcha gonna do? Shoot us both? And how would you explain that to Brando?"

Skull lowered the gun slightly.

"Chill." Keegan took another step forward. "I couldn't hang around and wait for you to wake up. I had to book it out of there. I ain't going back to prison," he said, keeping with his cover story. "Aren't you a little curious why Brando wants her dead? She don't look threatening to me. What's she got that he wants?" Keegan gave a jerk of his neck in Taya's direction.

"That's where you're gonna get yourself into trouble, Raptor. You don't question Brando about nothin'. Ever." Skull let out a low chuckle. "Oh, now I get it. You're turnin' her over to Brando yourself. Earn points by licking boots?"

Keegan fought to maintain a dull expression to hide his surprise. That option hadn't crossed his mind. It was better than the alternative of being a traitor. He'd work with Skull's narcissistic line of reasoning. "Whatever. I'm showing Brando I don't need no babysitter."

"So, why you out here playing possum?" Skull dangled the ketchup bottle from one hand, evidence he'd been inside the house.

Keegan shifted and glimpsed Taya out of the corner of his eye. He didn't miss the shake of her head, probably thinking, *I told you so. Think, Stryker.*

Skull waved his gun between them. "Don't matter. I already got proof you ain't who you pretend to be."

Keegan snorted. "That's just wack."

"We'll see." Skull patted the upper right pocket of his jacket, and Keegan spotted his nine millimeter nestled in the man's waistband.

What did Skull have hidden? *Keep him talking, get*

closer, then attack. "All that'll show Brando is you're losing your edge. Let's take this inside where it's warm."

Skull jumped at Keegan in a childish attempt to startle him, but he didn't flinch. Instead, crossing his arms over his chest, Keegan forced a bored tone into his question. "Finished?"

"Yep, just as soon as you prove you're not a double-crossing chicken."

Only one option. Accept the challenge. Keegan gave a jerk of his chin. "Name it."

"Kill the doctor. Here. Now."

Heart doing triple beats, Keegan searched for a retort. "Gimme back my piece or hand me yours." Once he had the weapon, he'd reverse this little tête-à-tête.

Taya gasped behind him.

"Nah, get creative." Skull hefted the pistol. "You've got three seconds."

Keegan turned and marched toward Taya, mouthing, *Don't move.* "I'm not playing your games." He reached out and grabbed her arm, tugging her closer. "You can follow or go on home, whatever you want."

Skull fired a round at the tree next to Keegan's head, raining chips of bark. Taya screamed and tried yanking herself free, but Keegan held tight, then gave her a firm tug to move behind him. She complied.

Keegan drilled his stare into Skull, unwilling to avert his gaze. "Are you out of your mind?"

"Nah, I'm crystal clear. I knew it! You're a cop."

"Gimme a break. You've known me for over a year." Keegan had to get Taya out of here.

He surveyed the space between him and Skull. Too far to tackle the man. He'd close the distance and yell for Taya to run into the woods. She'd have to hide there until he took out Skull. "If I'm a cop, then I've had you buffaloed all this time? Are you saying you're that stupid?"

"Don't call me stupid."

"You're not making any sense."

Skull gave a one-shoulder shrug. "Kill her with your bare hands or get outta the way so I can finish her."

Keegan sighed. "Fine. You win."

That brought a wide grin to Skull's mouth.

"You're right. I wanted to hand her over to Brando. I'm ready to move up. I deserve it. I've worked hard."

Skull's laugh was far from humorous. "You ain't earned nothin'. Brando wants her dead. And if you mess up, I'm killing you both."

Keegan allowed his anger to rise to a boil. "I don't take orders from you." In one motion he pushed Taya and commanded, "Run." Then bolted full speed at Skull.

The criminal hefted the gun and fired.

Keegan dodged to the side, the bullet narrowly missing him as he lunged, tackling Skull.

Skull's pistol came down hard on his back, sending a blast of pain through his kidney. Keegan jerked up and latched onto Skull's hand, driving it into the ground with all his strength. The impact forced open Skull's grip and he released the gun. But the criminal was quick and rolled them, gaining the top advantage.

Keegan thrust his knee into Skull's stomach, then wrapped his other ankle around Skull's boot to reverse their positions. He finished the attack with a headbutt, then drove his fist into Skull's nose.

Skull was unrelenting, forcing Keegan to hit him twice more to knock him unconscious.

He looked up, searching. Had Taya run away? "Taya?"

"I'm here." She emerged from the tree line and rushed to his side. "Is he dead?"

"No." Keegan yanked his nine millimeter from Skull's waistband and tucked it into his own. "Grab his gun."

She passed him the weapon, having already picked it up while Keegan fought Skull.

"Nice work. In the kitchen, top drawer, you'll find a rope. Bring it to me."

Taya nodded and rushed inside, returning seconds later with the rope. He tied Skull's wrists and ankles with double and triple knots, then dug into his jacket pocket and retrieved the man's cell phone. He scrolled through the calls and messages, landing on one to Brando. The message was still sending, based on the blue line across the top of the screen. The text read, Traitor Cop.

He cringed at the evidence of their ruse, and the most telling, one of him shooting the hole in Taya's hoodie.

Keegan switched the device to airplane mode, then dropped and crushed it with his boot.

"What are you doing?"

"He had pictures of us faking your death in a message to Brando. They're stuck in cyberspace for the moment and—"

"You think by destroying the phone, you can prevent them from sending," she concluded.

"Exactly."

"Will that work?"

"I turned off the internet connection, too, but I'm not sure."

"What do we do with him?" She pointed to Skull.

"Help me carry him."

Together they half carried, half dragged the unconscious man into the bathroom and crammed him into the standup shower. Keegan handed Taya Skull's gun. "Watch him."

Keegan had to move fast. He grabbed the burner phone dedicated to his communications with the traffickers and called Brando.

"Raptor. Is it finished?" Brando asked in greeting.

"Yep. Got proof for you, too."

"Excellent. I'll text you a date and time to meet me at the Camp." Brando referenced the abandoned youth organization summer camp at the edge of town that the traffickers used for their winter hangout.

"Why not now?"

"I trust you've handled everything. I'll be in touch."

Keegan disconnected and glanced at the clock: 4:35 a.m. They'd have to prevent all communication between Skull and the traffickers until Brando called.

As if responding to Keegan's thoughts, a thud echoed from inside the bathroom.

"He's waking up," Taya called.

Keegan hurried to the kitchen and tugged a roll of duct tape from the drawer. He snagged the towel off the counter. "Cover me. Whatever you do, keep your finger off the trigger and don't shoot unless I tell you." The last thing he needed was Taya getting trigger-happy and killing him.

"Got it."

Skull wriggled on his side like a walrus, but the confined space didn't give him much room to move. "You're dead! I'll kill you myself!"

"We can't have that." Keegan stuffed the towel in Skull's open mouth on his next rendition of threats and secured it with the duct tape. For good measure, he delivered a hand strike to Skull's neck, knocking him out again.

Double-checking the restraints, Keegan locked Skull in the bathroom. He tied a length of rope from the bathroom knob to the bedroom door, preventing Skull from escaping his mini prison.

In a swift tour, Keegan rushed through the home, collecting anything that would give away his true identity, including his ATF cell phone, and ushered Taya out the door. "Let's go."

How had Skull found them? The nagging worry weighed on Keegan's mind as they climbed into his SUV. He hit the garage button and backed out. Everything had changed. He had to get Taya to safety. Have Skull picked up and find somewhere else to hide before meeting Brando.

Keegan hesitated, lifting his foot off the gas. Maybe they should stay for a while. Buy time. But if Skull had contacted anyone and told them about Keegan's location, more of Brando's men could be coming. Why was Brando waiting to meet him?

Too many questions, and the most important mission now was to protect Taya. He hated to leave before his team apprehended Skull, but if he'd led any of Brando's men to them, they were in worse danger. They had to create distance and fast.

His safe house faded in the rearview mirror.

At the far end of the road, he spotted a pickup. "Must be how Skull got here."

Keegan pulled over and jumped out. Within minutes he'd cut the fuel lines, slashed all four tires and returned to the SUV. "That should delay him if he gets out of the restraints."

True to form, Taya interjected with a question. "What do we do now?"

"Have my boss pick up Skull when he comes for you."

Her next words surprised him. "I'd prefer to stay with you."

Why the sudden change? Taya's professed faith boosted his confidence, but concern countered the accolade. "I appreciate your trust in me, but I can't maintain my cover and continue working this case with you in tow."

She smirked. "You've got a rather high opinion of yourself."

"Excuse me?" Keegan's neck warmed with embarrassment for misunderstanding her comment.

"My desire to remain in your custody has nothing to do

with my personal confidence in your abilities. Although you've proven effective in your protection efforts."

Keegan snorted. "Thanks. I think. Still, it's best if you go with my boss." He lifted his work phone. "They'll get you away from this mess until I can arrest Brando."

"No!" Her emphatic tone jolted him. Just as quickly, she returned to her calm demeanor. "What I mean is, I cannot go with your boss."

"Lady, unless you've got something substantial requiring you to stay with me, I will transfer you into the ATF's custody," Keegan said, finishing their invigorating and thought-provoking debate.

She sighed. "It's clear I'm not safe and as you said, this Brando maniac will continue pursuing me."

"We've already established that." Maybe he could push her into telling him whatever she was hiding. "If I knew why Brando wants you eliminated, it would help. Is there something more you haven't shared with me?"

Several mile markers passed before she replied, "In my experience, fear is a powerful motivator."

That came out of left field, but he'd keep the dialogue going. "I agree."

"Why does Brando fear me?"

He hadn't anticipated that turnaround. She thought Brando was afraid of her rather than vice versa? Interesting. "You have something he wants."

A pause. "What else?"

Not a denial. Avoidance. "You tell me."

"I don't know him or have any association with these trafficking criminals."

Keegan scoured his brain. If she wasn't hiding anything—except his intuition said she was—what did Brando want from Taya? Skull's directions to eliminate her were clear. Whatever she possessed wasn't tangible. "Your knowledge," he blurted.

Taya nodded. "Right, but I've shared none of my suppositions."

Did the body contain evidence against Brando? "How long has the excavation been in process?"

"I'd only just begun."

"Have others hung around the site?"

"Yes, a few. However, Officer Folze has provided constant supervision, so the place is never unsecured. Only those preapproved may access the site. And I remain on the grounds at all times in my Winnebago."

He'd need a list of the people with possible connections to Brando. "Yet Folze wasn't there when Skull and I arrived."

She shrugged and her expression was almost sheepish. "That was my fault. I'd sent him away. The man's constant hovering is beyond annoying."

Skull had received a text before they'd walked up the valley. A message notifying them the officer had left?

"Did you see Officer Folze drive away?" Taya asked.

Keegan glanced at her. They were on the same wavelength too often. "Skull got the phone call and told me we had a new job. I assumed he meant meeting traffickers. When we trudged to the top of the hill, he motioned for us to stay by the Rhino Barn."

She nodded.

"I didn't realize you were there until we were standing by the building and I saw your LED work lights at the bottom. Once Skull said we were there to kill you, I had to go into action fast."

"So, you'd not been apprised of the body?"

"Nope."

"Is it a personal affront against me?"

"Could be. Or he wants to ensure you won't testify to the body's identification."

"Who is she?" Taya's question was soft, as if more to herself than him.

Keegan thought about the ring on Taya's dinette. The same one Patrice never took off. He worked the steering wheel, contemplating how much to share. "There's a possibility the deceased is undercover DEA Agent Patrice Nunes."

My stepsister.

Taya worked to maintain her nonchalance, disguising her amazement. Keegan's confession confirmed Patrice's video claim as a DEA agent. However, skepticism was Taya's middle name and she wouldn't abandon it without proper evidence.

Keegan's admission in no way proved his own ATF agent story. Was he a liar? A good guy gone bad? Had he been an agent at one time, but was no longer?

On the flip side, if he told the truth, he'd endangered and nearly sacrificed himself to protect her. No one had ever fought for Taya, and the concept nearly undid her.

So many questions, and she wanted answers. *Start with what you know.* "What evidence leads you to believe the victim is Patrice?"

"The butterfly ring you found. It's a custom piece Patrice's mother designed after her father passed away."

"And you're aware of this because—"

Keegan averted his gaze.

"You had a personal relationship with her." A statement, not a question, confirmed by his reaction. She'd hit pay dirt. A twinge of jealousy stole the sweet victory. What kind of relationship had Keegan had with Patrice?

Taya glanced down. She'd surmised the two butterflies symbolized a parent and child. Her heart squeezed. She shoved aside the uncomfortable emotions and returned to her inquisition.

A tiny niggling to relay the video details invaded her doubts regarding his true identity. If Keegan wasn't who he claimed to be, the videos provided her an upper hand with the authorities. Except, she'd lost the SIM card somewhere at Ashfall. Not lost, just misplaced and she'd find it again. Why hadn't she been braver and watched the rest? Did the footage reveal the killer? If the evidence implicated Keegan in the woman's death…

A flutter of fear set her nerves on edge and she glanced warily at him.

Her reasoning abilities returned. *Stop being paranoid. Consider all of the evidence.* He'd protected her from Skull. Twice. However, his deception might be woven in a plan to befriend her through heroic acts. Once he had the evidence, and she least expected it, would he kill her, too?

Knowledge was power and, at the moment, the only advantage Taya had over Keegan. The same knowledge placing her on Brando's kill list.

No, she wouldn't tell him about the video. Not yet.

Taya chewed on other possibilities. Was Patrice an old girlfriend? The contemplation brought no peace of mind. She glanced over at Keegan, gripping the steering wheel as though he hung on for dear life. Not the appearance of a prepared assassin.

"Why would someone want Patrice Nunes dead?"

He sighed. "I'm afraid there are too many possible answers. If she'd blown her cover or got too close to revealing Brando's identity, those reasons alone are sufficient."

Taya's mind jumped back to the video. Patrice claimed to be waiting for Brando. Had she identified him?

"I have to find out what happened to her. If she was compromised, maybe evidence pointed to a leak within the DEA or ATF."

Corruption wasn't unconscionable. "You think another agent turned on her?" Taya gave herself another mental berating for losing the SIM card before she redirected her irritation on blaming Keegan. She'd had it in her pocket until he grabbed her. Not something she'd be able to scold him about without confessing about the card.

"It's possible."

Appreciation for his candidness gave her pause. At least he didn't ruffle at the reality of law enforcement committing such atrocities. "You were aware of her undercover status?"

He nodded. "Not until later, but yes, the operation is a combined agency effort."

"When did you last speak to her?"

"A year ago. Shortly after the investigation began."

"Surely you communicate with your superiors? She with hers? Wear wires, all that type of thing?"

Keegan snorted. "Not even close. We absorb our cover roles. Sometimes we don't see family or friends for years."

Did he like living that lifestyle? Did he have someone waiting at home for his return?

Keegan continued, "We can't risk compromising our covers by talking to one another. Except…"

"Except what?"

"Skull dragged me to an impromptu meeting with a new buyer, who turned out to be Patrice. Her orders were to record the meeting and submit it to her superiors, but they never received the footage."

Taya gulped and faced the windshield, worried her reaction betrayed her secret. The meeting Keegan described occurred on the video she'd recovered from Patrice's pocket.

Tell him. No. Not yet.

However, the video was dated thirteen months prior and the state of decomposition correlated to the timeline. Without testing, Taya couldn't profess to be one hundred percent positive.

Something didn't cohere to the story. Did the government not care about their agents? Would they write off Patrice? "I don't mean to be callous, but if my friend had gone missing over a year ago, I'd be searching under every rock to find her. Perhaps if you'd started looking sooner? Why didn't your agencies do something, anything to find her?"

Keegan faced her, tension visible in his neck muscles. "What makes you think I haven't?"

Heat warmed her cheeks. Perhaps investing in a how-to-not-offend-others communication course would be wise. "My apologies. I only meant that after all the training and commitment the DEA put into molding Patrice, why ignore their missing undercover agent?"

He sighed. "No, you're correct in that respect. Unfortunately, they're not sure of her exact date of disappearance. It's not like we clock in and out every day."

"I see. Perhaps if I had more information about Patrice, the puzzle would come together faster."

"No offense, Dr. McGill, but it's a long story and not one I'm privy to sharing with you."

His use of her title inserted distance between them again. But she refused to be put off. "That's weak."

"It is what it is."

She softened her tone, reminded of the old adage regarding vinegar, honey and attracting bees. *Sweeten up your disposition.* "I understand the importance of confidentiality. However, the Antelope County sheriff requested my expertise to excavate the remains. Because I'm not directly involved with the investigation, I am an unbiased outside party."

He didn't respond and the mile markers blurred in her peripheral.

Finally, Keegan said, "Our agencies are working a cooperative case involving weapons and drug trafficking. Patrice was new to covert ops. I'd already infiltrated the traffickers and was deep undercover by the time I received word of her disappearance. At that time, the evidence pointed to her abandonment of the DEA."

"She betrayed the government?"

"That's what they said."

"What makes you think she didn't?"

He sighed and the long pause that followed had her wondering if he'd silently ended their conversation.

"Anything is possible, and maybe she had. But I knew Patrice. Her blood ran blue."

Taya shifted in the seat. "That's an enigmatic statement."

"She was devoted to her job."

"A poor cliché at best. Isn't every cop a dedicated member of society?" The comment came out a little sharper than she'd intended. "I apologize. That was uncalled for."

"Not a fan of law enforcement, I take it."

"I study people and behaviors. Social mores have little to do with my personal beliefs." She wouldn't go into her personal feelings. They needed facts to catch the killer. "Keegan, it stands to reason the person who doesn't want her identified is the same who benefits from her death."

"I appreciate your help, Taya, but I need to contact my CO. We have to get you to safety."

If only she'd reviewed the entire video. For the tenth time, she prayed, *Lord, that evidence is crucial in this case. Please hide it until I can get to it.* She'd return to the site first thing in the morning and search high and low for it.

But if Keegan turned her over to his boss, they'd haul her away into some kind of protective custody. No. She would identify the bones and get justice for Patrice Nunes. That was her job. Her calling. And it started with finding the SIM card and confessing the truth to enlist Keegan's help. She took a fortifying breath and exhaled. "I haven't been entirely forthcoming."

He glanced over at her a moment too long with what could only be described as *aha* written in his expression.

A smugness reserved for law enforcement? Doubtful. He had no clue what she would confess. The only way she'd get him to take her back to Ashfall was to tell him the truth.

"You were saying?" He quirked a brow at her.

"Focus on the road." This was it. Her last chess piece to move, but would it anger him? And if Keegan wasn't who he professed to be…

All the unknowns with large consequences made choosing difficult. She surveyed the inky surroundings. There was no place for her to run to. What irony. She'd have to be truthful to determine whether Keegan was trustworthy. "Patrice had swallowed a SIM card hidden inside a latex balloon."

"The kind used in cell phones?"

"And cameras. Before you and Skull burst through my motor home, I watched part of the first of two videos on the card. Patrice announced herself as a DEA agent, you and Skull entered her vehicle, and Skull told her Brando wasn't coming. The video was shot from a dashboard cam."

"The day Skull and I first met with her." A statement, not a question. Keegan slammed on the brakes and faced her. His expression dark, tone hard. "What else did you see in the video?"

Why had she told him about it? They were in the middle of nowhere. She had no place to run. She'd lost her advantage.

Keegan leaned closer, eyes drilling into her. "No more secrets. Tell me!"

Taya couldn't swallow over the rock stuck in her throat. With her back to the door, she worked her hand along the cold plastic, her fingers searching for the handle.

FOUR

Sheer desperation to get Taya talking increased Keegan's irritation. Her wide blue eyes blinked back at him, but she didn't respond.

Had Patrice recorded the elusive Brando's identity? Did the video reveal her killer?

Keegan calmed his voice, hope infusing his veins at the possibility of a new lead. He focused on parking the SUV and turned off the headlights. "We can't afford to waste any more time. What did you see?"

Taya lifted her chin, exuding confidence, though trepidation danced in her irises. She shifted, and her next words flew out in rapid succession animated by wild hand gestures. "I saw you and Skull enter Patrice's vehicle, but then I stopped the video. I was sitting outside near the site, but it got so windy. I turned off my camera and planned to finish viewing the footage in my motor home. Then Skull attacked me, you tossed me over your shoulder—"

"Breathe." He held up his hand.

Taya flinched, back against the door again.

"I wish you'd told me this from the beginning."

"I'm sorry." She sat stoic, shoulders visibly stiff, but her prior reaction spoke timidity.

Keegan softened his tone. "Look, I'm sure this has been

a nightmare for you. I hope I've proven by my actions and my word I'll do whatever it takes to protect you."

He caught a shimmer in her eyes before Taya blinked it away. "Thank you. I appreciate that."

A tenderness for the mysterious doctor filled his chest. His father said a man has the privilege of being a woman's knight in shining armor, though he'd meant the comment for romantic relationships. Keegan struggled to envision the intellectual Dr. Taya McGill wanting a rescuer.

He shoved away the impromptu thought and returned to the issue at hand. "We need that card. Is it in your motor home?"

Taya fidgeted with her hands; her voice barely audible. "Therein lies the problem."

Urgency flooded his veins. "Because…"

"I slid the SIM card into my parka pocket and lost it after you threw me over your shoulder. It has to be somewhere between where you parked the getaway car and my Winnebago."

It was missing? *No.* Frustration amped but blame wouldn't help anyone or solve the problem.

Think. "Could Skull have picked it up?" Even as he spoke, a new sense of foreboding came over him.

She shook her head. "No. I checked him at the house."

When? While Keegan was scrounging for his things? "We have to find it."

"I agree. Now you understand why you mustn't transfer me into the care of your boss."

Keegan considered Taya's request, unable to dispute her logic. Should he convey the information to Hawkins? Was the video the catalyst for Patrice's death?

"I need to call Hawk." Keegan withdrew his phone and hit the contact icon for Special Agent in Charge Otto Hawkins.

He answered on the first ring. "Stryker. What's wrong?"

"We have a problem." He continually scanned the area for any approaching danger and scooted away from Taya. With the phone pressed tightly to his left ear, he turned down the volume.

She leaned close in an obvious attempt to eavesdrop.

The road leading to the safe house snaked into the inky abyss where he prayed Skull remained unconscious and imprisoned in the bathroom.

"I'm listening," Hawk probed.

Keegan launched into an abbreviated synopsis of the evening's events, starting with Brando's orders to kill Taya at Ashfall and Keegan's attempt to fake her death.

Taya visibly shivered, though he doubted she was reacting to the cold temperatures. The SUV's heater blasted warm air. She hugged herself and nestled deeper into the passenger seat.

Hawk interrupted, "Two questions. Why was Dr. McGill there? And why does Brando want her dead?"

"She's a forensic anthropologist—"

"Isn't Ashfall a prehistoric site? A state park?"

If you'd let me finish. Keegan bit his cheek to keep from snapping at his boss. "Yes, sir, she's excavating recently discovered human remains. I believe Brando's trying to prevent her from identifying the body."

He couldn't say Patrice's name. She had to be alive. Somewhere. The body might be someone else. He clung to the sliver of hope dangling from a chain of denial.

Keegan continued his explanation and concluded with the final events leading to the unconscious Skull bound at his safe house. "Hawk, Skull can't get in touch with any of the traffickers or it'll blow everything."

"I understand. We'll detain him until after your meeting, but don't waste any time. What's your next move?"

"Returning to Ashfall."

"Why?"

"Following up on a lead. Dr. McGill advises the site has twenty-four-hour security courtesy of Gunner Folze, a game and parks officer." Keegan quirked a brow at her, confirming the information. She responded with a jerk of her chin.

"Seems to me if Officer Folze were competent at his job, you and Skull wouldn't have gotten to Dr. McGill in the first place."

No argument there. Folze never should've left the site. So why had he gone? An orchestrated event with Skull and Brando? "True. Give me a few to investigate, and I'll be in touch. We might need increased security. Will advise."

Several seconds ticked by before his boss said, "I've got a unit on the way to pick up Skull. They'll meet you and transfer Dr. McGill."

"The best course of action is for Dr. McGill to remain with me. Once I've met with Brando and delivered the proof of her demise, I'll contact you for Dr. McGill's pickup location."

Taya spun to face Keegan, vehemently shaking her head.

He held up a hand and mouthed, *Relax.*

"Why?" Hawk asked.

How was he supposed to answer without revealing the video? "I'll need her expertise at the grave site."

"And…" Hawk pressed.

"Brando won't stop pursuing Dr. McGill. Delivering the pictures will appease and trick him into believing she's no longer a threat. Then we'll make the transfer."

Hawk let out something between a laugh and a snort. Keegan caught the warning. "Negative. I recognize the importance of Dr. McGill's assistance and expertise, but there's no justifiable reason for her to remain with you when you deliver the information to Brando. Unless there's something you're not telling me."

Keegan swallowed hard. "Sir—"

"Stryker, stop dancing around the fire and give me facts."

Did he confess his personal desperation to protect Taya? Or his distrust in his team's credibility, especially if a mole existed? Neither gave Hawk what he wanted, but both satisfied Keegan's determination. *Less is better.* "If my information is correct, it might prove what happened to Patrice Nunes."

Hawk knew of the familial ties between Patrice and Keegan but for a reason he couldn't quite explain, Keegan didn't want Taya knowing. Yet. It was hypocritical to demand Taya's honesty while withholding information, but her life was already in danger. What good could come from knowing Patrice was his stepsister? It was irrelevant to Taya identifying the body.

Hawk sighed, impatience oozing through the line. "Stryker, I appreciate your dedication in searching for Nunes, but you've got to accept the evidence—"

"Please. Just a little more time." He didn't want to hear more about the evidence. The evidence was wrong. Patrice wasn't a deserter. And he wasn't in the mood to have this stupid conversation again. The video might provide a lead to Patrice's hiding place. The body at Ashfall had to be someone else. *Please, Lord, let it be someone else.* He cringed. Not exactly the proper prayer.

"I can't spare another agent for protection detail."

"No need. I've got it."

"Negative. Dr. McGill's transfer of custody happens before your meeting."

He sighed. "Understood. I'll call with a pickup location." Later.

"Okay. One more thing. HQ advised this operation ceases if we don't get a substantial lead on Brando within forty-eight hours. They're dissatisfied with the lack of progress."

Keegan exhaled. "They can't do that! This takes time.

I've just earned Brando's trust. He's finally communicating directly with me."

"HQ can and will do whatever they please. Zimmer and Steele have gone to bat for you on more than one occasion. They're fighting to keep you in the game until we crack this case. But you'd better produce something major. Fast."

Newly promoted Special Agent in Charge Wesley Zimmer was stationed in the Omaha office and held an equal rank to Hawk. Keegan and Hawk worked out of the Missouri office. Rarely did undercover ops remain in one location, and Brando's group had overlapped between the states.

Both Hawk and Zimmer reported to Randee Steele who had also been newly promoted to the ATF headquarters office in Denver.

Keegan valued Zimmer's mentorship and friendship over the years. Steele and Zimmer had proven to be huge advocates for Keegan regarding Patrice.

He wouldn't let down either of them. "Roger that."

Hawk disconnected.

Keegan faced Taya and the coldness in her eyes drove a twinge of concern through him.

"Hawkins will pick you up right before my meeting with Brando."

"Agent Stryker, you want me to trust you and yet again you've demonstrated deception."

He blinked twice as if clearing his vision would explain her accusation. "I beg your pardon?"

"Why didn't you tell him about the video?"

Keegan perused the area once more, flipped on the headlights and turned onto the road heading for Ashfall. "I'd like to see what we're facing before I mention it." Keegan redirected. "What do you know about Gunner Folze?"

"The man is a constant annoyance. I'd had enough of his incessant pestering to close for the holiday weekend.

We had words, and in a childish tantrum, he sped off in anger. I thought nothing of it."

Hawk hadn't mentioned Folze reporting Skull in the motor home. And why hadn't the officer reported Taya missing? Surely, he'd seen the dented door? Keegan withheld his questions, not liking the implications. A lazy man not concerned with Taya's safety or someone working with Brando?

"We don't want Folze catching on to our real reason for returning. We'll need a distraction."

Taya guffawed. "Folze is far from detective material. He's the path-of-least-resistance type. I'll say that the strictest security over the site is required as I'll be away for the weekend. The news will thrill him. He protested my staying at Ashfall and threw a conniption fit when I arrived in my Minnie Winnie."

"Good. If he asks, we'll just tell him you're looking for a personal item. No other details."

"Agreed."

They rode in silence the rest of the drive, each consumed by their own thoughts.

Taya sat up straighter, relief evident in her face as they reached the park entrance. Rounding the curve and ascending into the parking lot, the headlights beamed off the large Morton building sign boasting Rhino Barn.

He pulled up beside her Winnebago with its dented door hanging by a single hinge. Taya's prior reprieve evaporated into a taut jaw and narrowed eyes. Her fingers pressed into the dashboard and she scooted forward, scanning the area.

No other personnel or vehicles were around. Including Officer Folze.

The dig site lay beyond the main road. Perhaps Folze kept watch from there. Keegan's gut said that wasn't the case. He shifted into Park.

Taya voiced the same concerns, indignation in her tone.

"Where is Officer Folze? Why aren't police officers combing this place? The apathetic imbecile must have left assuming I'd gone away for the holiday weekend. Although had he bothered observing my Winnebago—with definite signs of a struggle—perhaps he'd have stuck around. I'm reporting him to his bosses and mine…" She threw off her seat belt and thrust open the door.

Concern wove through Keegan's mind, too. Folze had left the body unsecured.

Taya blasted past him, and he scurried to catch up. When they reached the site, she ducked under the yellow caution tape separating the area and lunged for the tarp, ripping it free. She stumbled back and Keegan caught her around the waist before she fell. "She's gone."

Taya jerked away from his hold, grabbed the tripod lights and turned them on, exposing the vacant ground.

Keegan prayed he'd heard wrong. "What?"

She spun and gestured at the grave. "Can't you see? It's empty! Someone stole her!"

"No." His whispered denial carried in the wind. He dropped to his knees, hands flat on his jeans. Icy gusts like frosty fingernails clawed at his face and neck.

The tarp flapped wildly. Mocking him.

The cold reality continued to probe him. If Brando had her, they'd never find and identify the body, proving it wasn't Patrice. He'd spend the rest of his life searching for her, always wondering if she was still alive.

The pain of losing his stepsister drove a spear through his heart.

He'd failed again.

Taya's heart wrenched at Keegan's brokenness. He'd shed no tears, never uttered laments, yet his sorrow was evident. She couldn't help but wonder, had Patrice been more than a coworker and friend? Had they been romantically involved?

She paused, conflicted as her normal air of suspicion shifted to compassion for the distraught man kneeling beside Patrice's empty grave. Leonardo da Vinci's quote sprang to mind and she mouthed the words, *The deeper the feeling, the greater the pain.*

Taya's disdain for injustice squelched what remained of her disbelief in Keegan's real identity. Would the loss of a DEA agent devastate a criminal? The sudden urge to defend him and recover Patrice's body rose within her. They had the same mission. And the same enemies.

The bright LED lights advertised their location. They needed to find the card and get out of Ashfall before the criminals returned.

She placed her hand on Keegan's shoulder and spoke softly, loath to interrupt his mourning. "Keegan. We should begin searching."

He jerked to look at her.

"What if Skull stole the body?"

Keegan shrugged. "I suppose it's possible but since Skull and I weren't aware of the remains, I doubt it."

"Right. I guess we should begin searching for the card, then." She stepped over to the lamp and lifted it. The light fluctuated, consuming the grave in darkness again.

Keegan trekked beside her in preoccupied, robotic steps, ascending the path to her Minnie Winnie.

With a last glance over her shoulder, she pulled open the door hanging by one hinge and stepped inside. The mess halted Taya in place and sucked the air from her lungs. She lingered at the top of the step well.

He leaned around her. "Taya, I'm so sorry."

"I suppose I shouldn't be surprised." She hoped her forced nonchalance concealed her distress.

Her gaze roamed the disarray. Every cabinet stood open,

and her laptop lay on the floor in scattered, small, irreparable pieces. Someone had ripped all the bedding from the mattress. They'd demolished her camera and shattered the screen. Mixed emotions swirled as she knelt and gathered the device. The perpetrators had removed her SIM card, and it lay broken beneath the camera. All of the crime scene photos destroyed. Gratitude for removing Patrice's SIM card—though it was missing now—helped with the shock of the devastation.

Did the person who'd done this know about the video? Focusing on the dinette, she searched for where Patrice's butterfly ring had been earlier.

Gone.

Had the intruders taken it?

Taya stepped over the debris, renewed by the mission. She ducked under the dinette, beckoned by the shimmer of silver. "Aha!" She snagged the plastic bag and backed out in an awkward crawl. "Not yet."

Keegan helped her stand, and she passed him the evidence bag containing Patrice's ring. "Where was it?"

"Wedged in the far corner between the base of the floor and the seat. It fell off the table when I tried to grab it earlier. Whoever did this damage must have missed it."

He inspected the contents, then pocketed the bag in his coat.

Taya shook her head and held out her hand. "You can't keep that."

"Just for now."

She relented and retrieved a flashlight from the floor beside the kitchen counter. "Let's find the card."

A fresh gust of wind met them outside, forcing Taya to zip up her parka while Keegan jogged to his SUV. He emerged, holding a flashlight. Together they used the grid pattern common to law enforcement, moving in synchronization and methodically scanning the ground from left to right.

"The card is bronze but it's contained in a small plastic case so it might blend in with the dirt," she advised, undeterred by the weather elements. "Please God. Please God." The mantra propelled her down the hill toward the grave.

The deep rumble of Keegan's whispers drew her attention and she studied him but dared not interrupt. He prayed, too?

Lord, bring justice for Patrice or whoever was buried here. Taya surveyed the area and a fresh rush of anger coursed through her at the crude disruption. The gaping hole ripped wide spoke of a quick excavation with no respect to the person or the evidence they'd destroyed. She peered inside and an object caught her attention. Taya knelt and dug out the partially exposed bullet casing.

"What'd you find?" Keegan dropped beside her.

She held up the casing and his jaw tightened.

"They shot her?"

"Yes," she said, omitting details in a compassionate effort to cushion news. She'd not officially confirmed a gunshot wound as the cause of death, but that was the awful reality. As a law enforcement professional, he'd piece it together, though nothing lessened the hurt regarding the crucial evidence.

"Why steal the body and leave the casing?" Keegan asked.

Taya sighed, conceding to give him more information. "I don't believe the thief realized it remained lodged inside the skull."

Keegan winced. "I'll get it to the ATF ballistics lab when we meet with Hawk."

She nodded and pocketed the casing. "Allow me to log the evidence first," she reminded him.

"Right."

Taya closed her eyes for a two-minute reprieve, battling exhaustion as she entered her twenty-fourth hour of being awake. The mini respite helped, and she appreciated Keegan watching over her. There was comfort in his protective presence, though she'd not admit it to anyone, especially him.

She focused again on the scene and scanned the area with her flashlight, illuminating a footprint.

"Find something?" Keegan asked.

"Give me a second. Keep searching."

Without waiting for his response, she scoured the earth, excitement building, as she made her way up the hill, then back to Keegan.

"Okay, what's going on?"

"See this?" She pointed to the first footprint.

"Yeah…"

"I inspected the grounds, paying special attention to places marked by the impressions of footwear. I've discovered five shoe imprints."

"Indicating five different people."

"Exactly. However, we need to factor in our own footprints."

Keegan stepped to the side and she knelt, studying his impression.

"See here? Your boots leave linear wiggly marks, which eliminates you from the group. Mine are smaller. Notice the triangular pattern in the center?" She pointed to the dirt. "I also walk on the balls of my feet."

"That's solid evidence of three other intruders on the grounds."

"Right. One of which includes Officer Folze."

"The devastation inside your motor home resulted from a struggle. Folze could've scared off the intruders."

Taya guffawed and stood, meeting his eyes. "I think the greater likelihood is Officer Folze arrived, saw I was gone and assumed I left for the weekend. He pushed me to go home, whining about his holiday plans. He doesn't understand how exhumations work."

Keegan faced the motor home. "But he couldn't have ignored the mess. And if he showed up when Skull was unconscious, why didn't he call it in? Or arrest Skull?"

Taya grunted. "From the little I know about Officer Folze, he doesn't strike me as an incognito warrior. Furthermore, he doesn't relish hard work. If he arrived here after my motor home's decimation, he most likely fled in fear. Plus, in his laziness, he wouldn't want to fill out an incident report."

"Well, that explains a lot. Just a guess here, but I take it you don't have a favorable view of Officer Folze?"

She shrugged. "His behavior is nothing if not consistent in our interactions. Even if I've judged him incorrectly, he'd be in trouble for leaving the site unsecured."

"Good point."

Taya knelt beside a boot impression. "Based on the depth and size, I'd say this belongs to Folze. He's a large man and I recall him wearing cowboy boots."

She paused and studied Keegan's response. Was she stating the obvious? Did he view her assessment as an insult or an attempt at flaunting her knowledge? No. He'd learned these factors in his academy training. He didn't appear offended and he didn't stop her.

Was it possible he valued her opinion? That would be a new development.

"What else?"

"Unfortunately, the impressions end here because the ground slopes into long grass and small patches of cracked and frozen snow."

Scanning the grave, she felt her heart sink again. She stood and continued toward the valley.

"I'm not sure it's safe for us to—"

"We're not done looking," Taya interrupted, resuming the same careful grid pattern across the frozen land to where they'd driven off in Skull's car earlier.

Neither spoke as they trekked back toward the motor home and Taya's determination waned. The card was gone. Either discovered, stolen or buried under careless footprints. She leaned against the Winnebago. "It didn't disappear. Did the intruders know about the video?"

Keegan turned off his flashlight. "Where'd you say you found it?"

"Near the thoracic vertebrae."

He quirked a brow.

"Sorry, near her ribs," Taya clarified. "She'd hidden the card in a balloon and swallowed it."

Keegan nodded. "Latex doesn't break down with stomach acids so she'd knew it'd be safe there."

"Exactly. Whoever did this might've stumbled upon the card I'd dropped out here. If they watched the footage, even the small portion I viewed, they'd know her real identity."

"Or the killer's identity." Keegan turned and faced her. "Let's check inside once more. Maybe you lost it when I tried to pull you through the window."

She led the way into the Winnebago, moving straight to the sleeping quarters where he'd shattered her window. Her foot crunched on something. She knelt and lifted her phone lying beside a chunk of broken glass. "Found my cell."

"Does it still work?"

Taya held it up for him. "Doubtful. They smashed it beyond repair." She dropped the device on the bed and moved to gather an evidence bag for the bullet casing. She logged and pocketed it. "What do we do now?"

Keegan shook his head and swiped a hand over the back of his neck. Palming his cell phone, he glanced down. "Pray."

"Okay."

Trepidation hung in his next words. "I have to report the theft of the body to Hawkins and deal with the consequences."

FIVE

Keegan's finger hovered over Hawk's contact icon.

"I'll keep looking while you make your call," Taya said, slipping out the door.

Doubtful she'd find anything, but her unrelenting attitude was admirable. He moved to the doorway, keeping Taya in his visual and did what he dreaded most.

Hawk answered on the second ring. "Stryker."

"Sir, we have a major problem."

"Yes, we do." His CO's voice was thick with a no-nonsense edge.

Keegan rushed on. "We're at Ashfall. Someone stole the body. Please question Skull to see if he did it."

Hawk spouted a creative word that would've sent Grandma Stryker reaching for a bar of soap. "I thought you said the game and parks officer provided twenty-four-hour security."

"Apparently, Gunner Folze has fallen short on the job. Or he's missing, too."

"Fantastic. This night just keeps getting better."

Keegan paused, confused. "Sir?"

"My contact discovered Skull in the bathroom as you said."

Keegan exhaled the breath he hadn't realized he'd been holding. "That's the first good news I've heard—"

"Dead."

"What?" Keegan pressed the phone tighter against his ear. His eyes remained on Taya actively searching the grounds.

"DOA. Hog-tied with a single gunshot wound to the back of the head. Execution style. I don't have to explain why that's a problem, Stryker."

Keegan paced in front of the Winnebago door, never losing visual of Taya. "Whoa. No way. I never hog-tied Skull. I told you, I knocked him out, restrained and locked him in the bathroom. If I'd shot him, I would've said so. He was alive and unconscious when we left."

"Did you fire your weapon?"

Keegan squeezed the skin at the base of his head, replaying the events in his mind. "Yes, but only to create the bullet hole in Taya's clothing for the sake of the picture. Skull fired several shots at us, though."

"Then they'll find GSR on his person."

Gunshot residue. *And on mine.* "Why would someone kill him?"

Did Skull's phone send the pictures and text message even after he had destroyed it? Did Brando know they'd faked her death? If so, how? The deceit placed Keegan on Brando's kill list. If the traffickers were onto him, he was a dead man. But if the pictures didn't send, there was only one way to know for sure. The meeting was his last chance to identify Brando.

Hawk continued, interrupting Keegan's thoughts. "I don't doubt you, but this is a huge problem. You know the procedures. Surrender your firearm for ballistics testing and come in for questioning. The evidence doesn't lie."

The same thing he'd said about the evidence against Patrice. But sometimes, evidence did lie.

Keegan ran his hand over his hair and paced a deeper path in front of the lingering Winnebago door.

"Stryker, the evidence isn't in your favor. A self-defense shot is justifiable but an execution-style murder…not so much."

"Why do I need a defense? I'm telling you, I left Skull alive and unconscious." Keegan mentally inventoried the last couple of hours. Hadn't he grabbed all of his guns before leaving the safe house? Hadn't he grabbed Skull's 1911, too?

He rushed to his SUV, throwing open the rear door and searching for the weapons. "Sir, I have all my firearms and Skull's."

"They found the murder weapon at the scene. If your fingerprints are on it—"

"Anything they found was planted by the killer."

"Stryker, we'll sort out the details later."

"I didn't do it!"

Taya spun to look at him, eyes wide. He held up his hand so she wouldn't rush back to him.

Once he submitted to questioning, she'd be an open target. Even if they put her into protective custody, Brando would never stop hunting her. He had to finish this for both their sakes. "Let me meet with Brando first."

Hawk sighed into the phone. "Turn yourself in or I'm coming for you."

"I'm only asking for a little more time. Brando's trying to frame me or flush me out."

"Then you'd best stay under the radar. You've got one day."

Keegan understood. Hawk had to arrest him. "I'll keep Dr. McGill safe until after the meeting." He'd find a way, whatever it took.

"Do you want Dr. McGill's blood on your hands? You can't keep her with you. It's too risky."

"You're right. I'll handle it." *Just not the way you want.*

Keegan had no intention of passing Taya off to someone else, and he didn't have time to argue with Hawk.

"Good. We never had this conversation."

"Yes, sir." Keegan walked toward Taya.

"Get out of there. If the thieves return, you can't risk Dr. McGill's safety."

"Affirmative." Should he tell Hawk about the video?

As if he heard Keegan's internal question, Hawk asked, "What lead are you following?"

Keegan neared the emptied grave site where the tarp flapped wildly. He glanced down, enraged. Until he had more information, he wouldn't release the details about the card. "I thought we might find an answer to why Brando wants McGill dead. Maybe something about the body's identification, but I didn't find anything helpful." No lie there.

"Make the best use of the time you've got left. At the moment, your alias, Raptor, is the prime suspect in Skull's murder."

Keegan faced an impossible choice. Normal department protocol required he undergo an internal investigation to prove the shot was necessary. No execution-style kill was justified, which meant disciplinary action and possible jail time. If he remained undercover, he'd be charged as an ex-con with a parole violation and incarcerated to keep in character with his role. Either way, they'd remove him from the case and he'd lose the opportunity to identify Brando. Worse, he'd never find Patrice's killer. "I understand." The only words he could form.

Hawk disconnected.

Keegan studied the cavernous hole beside him. How many times could he fail Patrice?

In life.

In death.

Taya touched his arm. "Did your boss take care of Skull?"

"He didn't get the opportunity."

Her eyes widened, and she frantically looked around. "He got away?" She surveyed the countryside past Keegan, no doubt fearful she'd spot the tattooed criminal storming them any second. No worries there.

"Worse. Hawkins found Skull—"

"Oh, that's good news." Her shoulders relaxed.

"—dead."

Taya gasped. "But I saw you. You rendered him unconscious. Didn't you? You didn't kill him. He was alive, correct? Or did you—"

Keegan shook his head. "I only knocked him out, but he had a fatal gunshot wound when Hawk found him."

She blinked several times. "You never fired your pistol!"

"Unfortunately, the agency doesn't see it that way. My alias is the prime suspect, wanted for questioning."

"Don't you have some kind of immunity as an agent?"

"It's complicated." He didn't want to go into the details with her. "We need to get out of here. Whoever trashed your Winnebago might return."

"Shouldn't we call the police? Wait for them to arrive and give our statement?"

"Negative. I'm still undercover. We're on our own until I meet with Brando. And I have to find Patrice." He dropped to a squat, staring at the hole in the ground. "I have to find her."

Taya couldn't ignore the tremor in Keegan's voice whenever he mentioned Patrice. Her heart ached for him, and she shook her head, frustrated at the unfair accusation he faced.

She didn't understand. Even if he'd shot Skull—which he hadn't—wasn't that a necessary quandary of his job? He'd never treated the maniacal criminal in the manner he deserved, though Skull had provided multiple opportunities.

The distant glimmer of headlights on the main road caught Taya's attention.

Keegan must've seen them, too, because he turned. "We have to go now."

"What if it's the police your boss notified?"

"Let's not chance it. Besides, remember I'm on the wanted list, and I don't have time for bureaucracy slowdown. I have to make my meeting with Brando."

They jogged back to the SUV and climbed inside. Keegan started the engine but didn't turn on the lights. He raced out of Ashfall via the valley with expert precision and turned onto the highway in the opposite direction of the oncoming vehicle.

Taya's fingernails dug into the armrest but she refrained from speaking. Her gaze bounced to the side mirror. Watching for the vehicle.

Keegan sped toward a country road and made another turn. Only then did he flip on his headlights. The hasty escape worked based on the fact no one appeared to be following them.

After the next detour onto a major highway and no sign of the other car, relief flooded Taya, and she settled back into the seat. "Now what?"

"Let's prepare for my meeting with Brando and grab some breakfast." He gestured toward the sky where soft pastels edged over the horizon indicating the rising sun.

Food didn't register on Taya's need list at the moment but she couldn't remember the last time she'd eaten. And coffee was a must.

Questions pelted her brain, and she was too tired to ask them. Instead, she focused on the scenery. This wasn't an area she'd visited before, but that wasn't saying much. Rural

Nebraska had many small towns with populations of less than a couple hundred.

Taya assumed Keegan would go to a convenience store. Not that she'd seen one on the roads they'd traveled. Her pulse picked up when he pulled onto Highway 14 and they passed a sign indicating the next town was Verdigre.

"Is it safe to return to Verdigre?" she asked.

"We won't be going to my not-so-safe-house." He grinned at her. "Just to a mom-and-pop bakery on the edge of town. We'll grab breakfast and get back on the road. There's nothing else nearby open this time of day in the direction we're headed. The place is older, without surveillance cameras, unlike a gas station."

Taya glanced at the clock. It wasn't even six o'clock. Keegan turned off the highway and onto the main thoroughfare leading through the town where the blackened storefronts of small abandoned shops bordered the two-lane street.

"Are you sure they're still in business?"

"Yep. They're only open in the morning when the kolaches are fresh."

He parked in front of a window outlined in Christmas lights. A black-and-white-striped tin awning hung above the entrance and Fresh Kolaches was written on the glass in colorful paint.

"I don't mean to sound uninformed, but what's a kolache?" Taya asked, trailing him.

"They're like danishes." Keegan held open the door and they entered the small bakery.

The delightful aroma of baked goods mingling with coffee met her and she inhaled deeply. Christmas carols chimed from a speaker behind the counter. The space was compact but big enough for a large waist-high glass countertop, filled with rows of delicious high-sugar delicacies. Taya wouldn't normally indulge in the wonderful danishes, but this morning, she couldn't wait to try one. Her stomach growled in protest or agreement. Hard to say which.

Keegan glanced over at her and warmth radiated up her neck. He'd clearly heard the sound, too, but graciously didn't make a big deal. Desperate to create space should her stomach offer another loud opinion, Taya walked up to the counter.

A fiftyish woman, short and stout with a mass of gray curls framing her round face, greeted Taya with a wide grin. "Good morning. What can I get you?"

"Coffee with lots of cream please."

The clerk placed a hand on her hip and stepped back. "Oh, honey, surely you came for more than that. Mama's kolaches are world famous."

Somehow Taya doubted the claim, but the woman was endearing. Keegan moved to the back of the bakery where a cooler held sodas and milk.

"Hmm, you need sustenance to hold you for the day. Got a sweet tooth?"

Taya grinned. "Yes, ma'am."

That seemed to please her. "Well, then, I have just the thing for you. Been dying to try out this new machine we got. Let me whip up something that'll warm you and exceed your sugar count for the month."

Without waiting for Taya's agreement, she turned her back and prepared the concoction. A paneled swinging door like the ones in her father's old Westerns separated the areas. Clatters and the pleasant humming of a man's voice echoed from beyond the doorway where Taya assumed the baking occurred.

A cool rush of air caused her to turn around. A man entered and paused. His dark eyes seemed to survey her as he blocked the exit.

An uneasiness washed over her, and she glanced at Keegan, who appeared intrigued by his pastry selection.

Taya slipped to the side and studied the newcomer. He wore jeans and a heavy yellow-brown parka. Thick tan leather gloves covered both hands, and his unkempt over-grown beard hung to the middle of his chest. She detested facial hair. It reminded her of Jeremy's carefully groomed goatee. And anything Jeremy-related was unwelcome. A dislike for the man overtook her apprehension.

"Morning," the man said.

Taya blinked, realizing she'd stared a moment too long. "Good morning."

"Be right with ya, Earl," the clerk greeted.

"No rush, Mertle." Earl stepped closer and removed his gloves. He pulled a phone from his coat pocket and typed something.

Taya scurried to Keegan's side. He continued study-ing a taller glass display case filled with an assortment of circular colorful treats packaged in clear plastic bags. Ev-erything looked the same to her, but he appeared deep in thought about his selection.

Keegan grabbed one of the Styrofoam plated offerings and passed it to Taya, then glanced down at the soda he held. "Oops. Diet. Can't have that." He walked back to the refrigerated section and withdrew two colas.

She returned her attention to the newcomer. He'd gone around the counter and was helping himself to the cof-fee maker.

"Oh, you!" Mertle chastised with a chuckle. "Get out of here."

Earl laughed. "I'm helping you out." He walked around the counter and leaned against it. "Can I get two bear claws?"

His phone chimed and he checked it, then said, "Well, that's good news."

"Trying something new?" Mertle removed two bear claws from the case and placed them in a white bag.

"Yeah, I'm living on the wild side today. Man cannot live on kolaches alone." He paid for his items and addressed Taya, "However, if you've never had them, you need to try the raspberry ones."

Taya held the plated package, unsure how to respond. "They look delicious," she finally said.

"Oh, no, honey, I have a fresh raspberry batch," Mertle chimed in.

Taya opened her mouth, intending to politely decline the offer, but the man lifted his hand. "They're the best. Make sure they get a couple, Mertle."

"Will do." She waved at him.

"Have a great day." He took a bite of his bear claw, leaving a few lingering crumbs dangling in his beard, and exited the bakery.

Taya sighed. Maybe Keegan liked raspberry.

When the door closed, Mertle whispered, "Earl's here daily. Thinks he owns the place." She chuckled and disappeared into the kitchen area, returning seconds later holding a fresh package of kolaches. "Here, hon, take these. On the house."

Taya took the second platter with two perfectly round pastries with bright raspberry-colored fruit filling.

"Oops, almost forgot your drink." Mertle set a cardboard cup on the counter.

"What did you order?" Keegan joined her, the colas tucked under his arm and a large platter of various kolaches in hand.

"I'm not sure what Mertle made me." She glanced at his breakfast beverage choice. "Not into coffee?"

"Nope." He grinned. "But I appreciate caffeine."

Mertle stated the total. Keegan paid for the items with cash while Taya snagged several napkins and followed him outside.

Once they'd entered the SUV and gotten settled, Keegan started the vehicle.

"As an ATF agent, aren't you supposed to be a skilled observer?"

"I am."

"But you never even looked at the guy who came in."

"You mean Earl? What makes you think I didn't see him?"

Taya considered his question. A good observer wouldn't be obvious.

"He wouldn't win any fashion awards, but he wasn't carrying a weapon. Besides, he seemed pleasant enough with Mertle. I've never seen him around here, but that's not saying much. We're near Chief Standing Bear Bridge."

Taya lifted an eyebrow.

"It's a bridge over the Missouri River, connecting Nebraska and South Dakota about fifteen miles from here."

"I stand corrected."

He grinned. "I think we're okay for now but I'll feel better once we get to a nondisclosed location. We can eat our breakfast there. I'll also call a buddy to help us. We need extra eyes while I meet with Brando." He started made a U-turn in front of the bakery, then headed to Highway 14. "Oh, Earl drives a light blue king cab dually."

"How do you know that?"

"I saw him get into it when we paid for our food."

As they departed the small town of Verdigre, Taya noticed a large pickup closing in behind them. He remained at a distance. "Um, Keegan. You mean *that* dually?"

He glanced at the rearview mirror. "Yep."

"Think our friend Earl from the bakery just happens to be going in the same direction as us?"

"Any other day, I'd say yes. I'll take a slight turn and see if he follows."

Taya sat back in her seat and placed the coffee in the drink holder, freeing her hands.

Keegan rounded the corner, and the pickup followed. The engine roared as Earl increased speed and continued gaining on them.

"He's getting closer." Unable to tear her eyes from the side mirror, she nonetheless tried to scoot out of view, concerned that Earl saw her reflection.

"Ya think?" Keegan snapped.

"What does he want?" Taya peered over the headrest.

"Probably not to ask how we liked the raspberry kolaches."

She glared at him. "Right."

Keegan reached into his jacket pocket and withdrew his phone, tossing it to her. "Call 9-1-1 and report a reckless driver. Give them the make, model and license plate."

Taya clutched the phone and twisted around in her seat, spotting the dirty license plate.

Earl moved closer again, providing a better visual of the plate, but another thrust forced the phone from Taya's hand. It landed with a thud on the floorboard.

She had to remove her seat belt to retrieve the device. The pickup hit them again, throwing her into the dashboard. Taya got back into her seat and snapped her belt.

The SUV's tires screeched as the force sent them swaying across the road and headed for a metal mile marker.

Keegan regained control as Taya struggled to hit the correct numbers. She pressed the phone against her ear, her gaze fixed on the side mirror.

"9-1-1, what's your emergency?"

"Someone's trying to kill us!"

SIX

Keegan maintained one eye on the rearview mirror while searching for a place to break free from Earl's violent ramming. They lacked horsepower to outrun the dually, and strength to prevent the maniac from forcing them off the road.

His grip tightened on the steering wheel, every muscle taut. *Come on. There has to be a spot... There!* A bend ahead emerged like a beacon, sprouting an idea in Keegan's brain. The SUV had the advantage of agility over torque.

Lifting his foot slightly off the accelerator, he allowed Earl to line up behind him. The diesel's roar increased; a good indicator he'd taken the bait.

When the pickup was within inches of the SUV's bumper, Keegan swerved to the left and slammed on the brakes right before the bend, forcing Earl past him.

Keegan swung around and accelerated in the opposite direction. Brakes screeched from behind. Glancing in the mirror, he grinned at the bright red lights, no doubt a direct reflection of Earl's anger. It would take him significant adjusting before he'd pursue again.

"Excellent maneuver!" Taya complimented.

"Thanks, but it's not over yet. We need to disappear." Keegan took the first turn onto a familiar county highway, then three more detours until he reached an unpaved lane.

Taya twisted in her seat, peering out the back window. "I don't see him following us."

"We lost him." *For now.* "Would you hand me my phone please?"

She passed over his cell, and Keegan parked behind a grove of trees, maintaining visual on the road. As much as he enjoyed the mini solo tour of duty, it was time for backup. Bear Nichols came to mind, the only person he counted on outside his ATF team. The man had more special ops experience in his little toe than Keegan would ever attain.

He dialed, and the line rang four times, deflating his hopes.

He prepared to hang up just as Bear answered, "Stryker, you know what time it is?"

Keegan glanced at the dashboard clock: 8:35 a.m. "It's not that early."

"It is when you're retired."

"Sorry, man, but I could use your help."

"Name it."

Keegan exhaled relief at Bear's gravelly commitment. "It might place you on the wrong side of the law."

"Never been an issue before."

He chuckled. "I'm undercover and need outside backup."

"What about your team?"

"Possibly compromised."

"Roger that."

Taya shifted in her seat, eyes glued out the window.

"I also have a witness requiring a temporary bodyguard."

Her gaze snapped to him, and he held up a finger. She responded with an eye roll.

"You want me to be your bodyguard?" Bear asked.

Keegan chuckled. "Not for me. Dr. Taya McGill. She's

a forensic anthropologist working on a case in Ashfall. She's on Brando's list."

"That pathetic excuse for a living brain donor again? Now I'm really in. Whatever puts that loser behind bars. Where are we meeting?"

Bear's indisputable gift with words brought levity to the intense situation. "The abandoned school building in Brunswick."

"It'll take me about four hours to get there."

"No problem, a little downtime will help while I line up a few details."

"On my way."

Keegan disconnected.

"Bear? Is that his real name?" Taya asked.

"Nickname. He's a friend."

"Why are you requisitioning a bodyguard for me? I'd prefer to stay with you."

"I can't risk taking you to the meeting or leaving you alone."

Taya snapped her gum, her disapproval registering. But this was one area she didn't get an opinion.

Keegan glanced at his phone. How had he missed a text from his confidential informant, Wanda? He opened the message. Need to talk.

He replied, When?

9:30 Jensen farm

What did she have for him? Maybe info on Skull's murder? He wouldn't have time to take Taya to Brunswick before meeting Wanda. He replied, OK.

"We're taking a minor detour," Keegan said. He'd have to prep Taya, and she'd have to remain out of sight or Wanda might panic and not tell him anything.

"Why?" Taya asked.

"I have a CI—" he began.

"—confidential informant?"

"Yes. Her name's Wanda. She's asking to meet right away. If she spots you, she'll clam up. Sorry, but you'll have to jump in the back and stay down."

"If you say so."

They drove in silence until Keegan neared the abandoned Jensen farm. He pulled over and Taya moved to the rear seat. He covered her with a light blanket, disguising her small frame.

"Ready?"

"I suppose."

As he approached the farm's entrance, Keegan scanned the property. He'd arrived early as a precaution. The barn at the far north side provided cover and an alternative road into the pasture should he require a speedy escape. He pulled up and parked, watching.

"Is she here?" Taya asked.

"Not yet. Don't move. I'll clear the barn."

"You're leaving me alone?"

"I'll lock the doors and return in less than five minutes."

Keegan exited the SUV and hit the door locks. It wouldn't take long to clear the lone standing building.

The lack of wind tempered the cold morning. He tugged his coat tighter and made his way through the decrepit barn, leaning heavily to one side. Rotting hay and old equipment filled the space. The farm, like many abandoned rural Nebraska properties, had been sold to a corporate farming agency who didn't need the outdated equipment.

An engine drew Keegan outside, and he spotted the approaching vehicle. He unlocked the SUV with his key fob while sprinting the short distance and slid behind the wheel.

"Everything okay?" Taya asked.

"Yep. Now remember, whatever you do, don't move or make a sound. Wanda's as skittish as a rabbit."

"Okay."

Sure enough, the familiar beater made its way down the road. She parked beside him on the passenger side and got out, then climbed into his SUV.

Wanda wore a much too thin jacket, insufficient for the bitter winter cold. She shivered and settled into the seat. "Sorry to text so early, but I've got news," she said.

Keegan turned up the heat, blasting warm air into the SUV. "What's up?"

"Skull's dead."

He worked to evoke a shocked expression. "What? How? I just saw him last night." None of it a lie.

"That's all I know." She wanted something else, but probing her to talk was a delicate operation.

"Keep your ear out and text me if you hear anything else."

She nodded.

"How're you doing? Still clean?"

Wanda's methamphetamine addiction had served as the catalyst for destroying her life. She'd lost custody of her infant daughter and had racked up felony charges to support her habit. Keegan recruited Wanda after confirming her desperate acts weren't a criminal lifestyle she wanted to continue. Losing her daughter had been the wakeup call she needed.

She knew his true identity and she'd proven herself trustworthy. Serving as his CI helped reduce her sentencing and gave her the slim possibility of regaining custody. The hope of getting her daughter back ensured her cooperation, giving them both a win-win situation.

She shrugged. "Brando says there's a way to beat the system."

"Brando's a liar. The best thing is for you to get sober and find a job. Prove to the judge you can handle being a mom."

"I make more working for Brando. I can do it without using, too."

"Wanda, look at me."

She glanced up slowly, meeting his gaze with her blood-shot, tired brown eyes. Years of drug abuse had aged her twenty-year-old face with lesions and rotted out her teeth.

"You cannot trust Brando. He's trying to keep you in his grip. You're doing great by helping me. Where's your reminder?"

Wanda reached into her jeans pocket and removed a small picture of her daughter.

Keegan pointed to the beautiful child. "Do what's right for Molly. She needs her mother."

She looked down and nodded. "I can do all things through Christ which strengtheneth me," she quoted.

"Exactly. Rely on Christ's strength, okay? You're making progress every day you're sober."

A tear slipped down her cheek as she fingered the picture.

"When's the last time you ate or slept?"

She shrugged.

Keegan glanced at the coffee, sodas and kolaches. He lifted the platter and offered them to her, but she declined with a shake of her head.

"No, thank you."

"Wanda, I need a favor."

"What?" Apprehension covered her expression.

"I requested a meeting with Brando, and he said he'd get back to me. But it has to happen today. Can you help me by arranging the details with Brando?"

She nodded. "Okay."

Keegan dug into his pocket and pulled out cash. He placed it in her hand. "Take this. Buy groceries and a get a hotel for a few nights."

Wanda's lip quivered. "Thanks. I'm still learning 'bout

God, but if He's anything like you, He must be a good man."

Her words hit him with the intensity of a grenade. *Lord, I'm not worthy. Help me show her Your love.*

"I better go."

"I'll be in touch," Keegan promised.

Wanda didn't reply as she slipped from the SUV. She returned to her car and drove away.

Once she was out of sight, Keegan said, "It's safe."

Taya pushed back the blanket, and he caught a shimmer dancing in her crystal blue eyes. "You're a good man, Keegan Stryker."

If only Taya understood that no good deed recompensed his failure to protect Patrice.

Nothing he did would ever be enough.

Taya stared incredulous at the three-story redbrick building that had to be on a historical site list somewhere. The old abandoned school sat on the edge of town and seemed to grow more ominous as they drew closer, even with the morning light reflecting off what remained of the upper-level windows.

Keegan parked on the backside away from the view of the road.

"You want me to hide in there?" Taya sent up a silent prayer that wasn't the plan.

"Trust me. This is a fortress."

She didn't respond.

"It looks worse on the outside than it does on the inside."

"Even without a personal assessment, I'd say that's debatable."

She ignored Keegan's adorable lopsided grin. He busied himself gathering a pair of binoculars, which he hung around his neck, then grabbed a flashlight from the console. He pushed open the driver's door and stepped out, slipping his gun into the waistband of his jeans. Last, he tucked his soda bottles into his jacket pockets.

Glued in her seat by dread, Taya didn't move until Keegan approached the passenger side.

She reluctantly slid out of the vehicle. Then remembering the two packages of kolaches and her coffee, grabbed them before shutting her door.

He walked to the rear of the SUV and popped the hatchback. "Can you shoot?"

Taya hesitated. Technically, she hadn't fired a gun in years and the last time had been for fun using targets. How hard could it be? Something akin to riding a bike. Pride kept her from confessing her inadequacies. Besides, with Bear protecting her, she wouldn't need a gun anyway. "A little."

Keegan withdrew a pistol and handed it to her. "Only in an emergency and remember, the safety is on."

She nodded and tucked the gun into her waistband, mimicking him.

Boards covered most of the school's lower windows, but the remaining few revealed blinds hung askew.

"Local legend says the place is haunted," Keegan said.

Taya halted and glared at him with what she hoped conveyed her most dubious I-don't-believe-you-and-I'm-not-going-in-there look.

He laughed and tugged at her non-coffee-bearing arm. "You're a scientist, right? You don't buy into that stuff. But I view the legend as a benefit because it keeps intruders away."

"If you say so."

Keegan glanced up and gestured toward the structure. "Don't you love the architecture? And this construction is solid and dependable. Yep, you'll be safe here while I go to The Camp to meet Brando."

Was he trying to convince her or himself? Taya trailed Keegan to a single side door. A padlock prevented entry.

She paused and studied a long metal tube running from the third floor to the ground. "What's that? Resembles an antiquated slide."

"Pretty much. It's an old fire escape chute," Keegan said. Inserting a key, he removed the padlock and pushed wide the wooden door.

Taya shook her head. "After you."

He grinned and ducked under the overhanging cobwebs. Taya followed, gaze roaming the darkness. She jerked when the door slammed behind her, engulfing them in a wave of dust. Keegan flipped on his flashlight and led her through the narrow staff entry into the main hallway. The stuffy air hung thick and their footsteps echoed.

She stayed close beside him. "Why this place?" she whispered.

"Trust me, no one ever comes here. I put the padlock on six months ago. You saw it's still undisturbed."

Sweeping the light, Keegan illuminated the first-floor classrooms as they made their way through the hall. Taya hung back, hugging herself, unable to move into the ominous darkness.

Keegan must have sensed her absence because he turned and walked back to her. "Are you okay?"

She glanced up, still frozen. "I hate the dark," she admitted.

"Want me to carry you? Or would you prefer to hold my hand?" His grin was teasing, but she considered taking him up on both offers.

Instead, she shook her head. "I'm coming."

"We're almost there," Keegan assured, leading her through the blackness.

Gradually, their trek brightened courtesy of two rectangular windows high above the expansive foyer. Keegan moved to the left wall, where a massive wooden staircase cascaded elegantly from the floor above.

Upon closer inspection, Taya noted several broken steps with gaping holes. Her gaze traveled to the second- and third-floor landings that disappeared into the darkness. "Can't we stay on the main floor? Wouldn't that be safer?" She placed her hand on his arm to stop him from walking away.

"You'll have a great visual from the top. Be careful which steps you walk on. Some of them have rotted out but most are intact. Keep to the far sides where the stairs are the strongest. Follow me." He didn't wait for her so Taya schlepped behind him, cautious to step in his path to avoid her foot going through the wood.

When they reached the second floor, Taya studied the slivers of sunlight peering between uncovered sections of the tall window. Hallways on either side faded into gradually increasing shades of gray that merged into blackness at the far end.

Keegan led her to the right. "Most of the rooms are bare or filled with junk. There's no in-between." He pushed open the first door, groaning in disapproval.

Spears of light filtered in and Keegan shut off the flashlight. Taya studied the classroom, devoid of furniture. The blackboard still displayed the daily assignments in a teacher's elegant cursive.

They exited and moved farther down the hall but didn't stop to inspect each room.

Taya imagined children laughing, teachers instructing and the many lives that once filled this building. She detested the lack of sunlight, but couldn't deny her appreciation for the architecture. Even with the old musty smell, there was an endearing uniqueness to the school.

At the end of the hallway, Keegan turned on his flashlight and entered the last room. The covered windows prohibited sunlight, and his beam bounced off stacks of desks, file cabinets and other assorted junk.

"Why not clean this up and use it for historical purposes? Or repurpose it in some other way?" Taya asked.

Keegan shrugged. "Who knows? A shame, though. I think this old place has many years left to share."

She studied him, intrigued by his gentle thoughtfulness. The same characteristics had touched her heart as she'd eavesdropped on his conversation with Wanda.

They continued their tour to the third floor—a duplicate of the second—with only the sound of their rhythmic footsteps accompanying them. When at last they reached the top of the stairs, Keegan paused.

Taya's pulse increased and she strained to see what kept him from proceeding.

Finally, he moved across to a closed door centered in the hallway. He reached into his pocket, withdrew a key and opened the door. "The middle room has the best view."

"Of what?"

"Everything." Keegan entered and set his soda bottles on a teacher's desk at the front of the rectangular room.

Taya placed the kolaches, her coffee and the pistol beside his drinks. She walked the length of the area to the only window not covered by boards. "I'm still baffled at why we're hiding here. Why not a hotel?"

"We need to be invisible. Hotels have too many people."

She returned to the teacher's desk and wiped off a corner before sitting. "How do you know we're safe?"

Keegan joined her. "Sometimes I come here to relax and conduct surveillance. I have a great view of Brando's Camp from that window." He passed her the variety kolache platter. "However, if you've got a better idea I'm listening."

Taya shook her head. "Wish I did. What are the flavors?" She took the plate from him, diverting from his comment.

"Apricot, cream cheese and prune. The other package has raspberry ones."

She wrinkled her nose. "Prune?"

"Best ones. Don't knock it till you try it."

"You can have the raspberry ones. Not my favorite flavor, but the bakery clerk insisted and I didn't have the heart to tell her no." Taya withdrew an apricot pastry.

"I'm not a raspberry fan, either." He took a prune kolache. "Last chance. There's only one."

"No, thanks. Help yourself."

He slid off the desk and moved to the farthest window and, using the binoculars still hanging around his neck, peered out the broken glass covered in cobwebs and dust.

"Anything interesting?" Taya asked.

"No. It's too early. Brando's men don't move before noon. Which is why I meet Wanda in the mornings."

Taya considered asking her hundred and one questions about his confidential informant, but didn't want to be appear nosy. She'd only heard Wanda's voice and pictured an older woman based on the deep, raspy tone. "What does she look like?"

Keegan walked to her and withdrew his phone. He swiped at the screen and passed the device to her.

The woman staring back at Taya was nothing like she'd envisioned. The mug shot—which was never flattering anyway—took her aback. Long, scraggly dirty blond hair framed her gaunt and sunken face. Dark rings encircled her shadowed brown eyes and lesions covered her cheeks and forehead. A sadness seemed to hang over Wanda.

"She's had a hard life," Keegan said, taking his phone back. "I met her when I first went undercover in Brando's group. She lost her infant daughter after she almost OD'd on meth." He studied the phone. "I don't know. Something about her tore at my heart. I found a way to help her as long as she'd become my CI. She's done a great job staying clean even with Brando pushing her to use again."

"Does that happen often?"

"What?"

"Being moved by a troubled soul like Wanda."

Keegan shook his head. "That's the thing with law enforcement. It's a fine balance between discerning liars and cons to helping victims. I don't think rehabilitation works for everyone. But Wanda has a chance. She's got something to fight for and that makes a big difference."

Taya nodded. Keegan continued to impress and confuse her. Worse, he was tearing at her hard-hearted assumptions regarding cops. She bit into the kolache, surprised at the buttery crust and sweet fruit combination. "This is scrumptious."

"Glad you like them." He withdrew a second—cream cheese this time—and took a bite. "Dr. Taya McGill, we've got time to kill. Tell me about you."

"I'd prefer not use the term 'kill' if it's all the same."

"Sorry."

She shrugged. "No offense, Keegan, but I'd rather not chitchat. I'm exhausted."

"You're right. We need to recoup." He walked to a cabinet and retrieved a rolled sleeping bag. "Not fancy, but beats lying on the floor."

"You keep supplies?"

"Told you, I stay here and do surveillance sometimes," he said, unrolling it. Keegan whistled a familiar Christmas song.

"Hardly seems possible it's almost Christmas." Taya dropped onto the sleeping bag and leaned against the wall.

"Have a big wish list?"

She snorted. "Nope. I prefer to survive the holidays unscathed. However, I look forward to a new year."

"Oh, yeah? Are you a resolution person?" He took a swig of his cola.

"No. I like beginnings, though. Fresh starts."

"Christmas was always a big deal in our house. My dad dressed up as Santa Claus when I was young. Later, my stepmother, Ione, decorated every room and we had a massive tree."

"That must've been fun." Taya averted her gaze, not wanting Keegan to see her jealousy. Christmas festivities lost their appeal at the McGill home after *the incident*. She shook off the painful memories.

Keegan stared past her at the chipped blackboard across the room. "I haven't celebrated with my family in two years."

"Because of your job?"

"Yeah." A sadness lingered in his reply. "I'll be glad to go home."

Did someone wait for Keegan's return?

Why did it matter?

The perplexing answer consumed her thoughts. Keegan had drawn out a braveness she never knew she possessed. The glimpses of his tenderness for others morphed her view of law enforcement officers. Worse, he'd awakened her heart and that terrified her.

Asking questions about him would only solidify his departure and invite discussion about her personal life. And she wasn't willing to go there.

SEVEN

Keegan startled at his phone's chime and silenced the device before reading the text from Wanda. Meeting postponed.

What did that mean? He slid off the desk and walked toward the window where bright sunlight filled the room with warmth.

Soft rhythmic breaths carried from where Taya lay curled on the sleeping bag, one hand tucked under her cheek. He studied her youthful features, her pursed rosebud lips and small nose. Long blond hair cascading in waves to the middle of her back. Cute as a button, Grandma Stryker would say.

Taya McGill was beautiful, compassionate and intelligent. Even asleep, she appeared to be thinking. Why was she alone? What secrets was she hiding? She'd thwarted his questions.

For now.

Another text redirected his attention. This time from Bear. An hour out.

He palmed the phone, debating. Hawk warned that HQ's deadline hovered, and waiting wasn't a luxury Keegan possessed.

Resolute on his plan, Keegan stepped out of the room, careful not to wake Taya, and dialed Brando's number.

"What?" A familiar female voice he couldn't place barked through the line.

"It's Raptor. Need to meet with Brando."

A pause. "I'll call you back in five." She disconnected.

Keegan returned to the room where Taya sat rubbing her eyes. "Sorry, did I wake you?"

"No. How long was I asleep?"

He glanced at the clock on the phone. "Couple of hours." Plenty of time for him to run through a hundred different scenarios. "Feel better?"

"A little. That's almost a full night's sleep for me, anyway."

"Insomnia a regular thing for you, too?"

"Yes. What have I missed?" Taya ran her fingers through her hair, then got to her feet and walked to the desk where her coffee cup sat.

"I'm waiting for Brando to call back."

She took a sip and cringed. "It was much better warm."

"Have a soda." He offered, pointing to the plastic bottle beside the kolaches.

"Never drink the stuff. I'll pretend I'm drinking a Frappuccino." She grinned and crossed the room to the window, peering out. "It's a pretty day."

The phone rang, and she spun to face him.

Keegan pressed his finger against his lips. "Raptor."

"Dusk. The Camp." The caller disconnected, giving him no chance to respond.

"Meeting's at dusk," he said.

Taya's eyebrows peaked. "Why not a specific time?"

"Who knows? Guess we're stuck here for a while." He dropped onto the teacher's desk. "I've been thinking. We need a contingency plan."

"Why?"

Keegan exhaled. "Plan for the worst, hope for the best."

"Oh."

"If Brando doesn't buy our ruse, and you're forced into witness protection, is there anyone he'd go after to hurt you?"

Alarm combined with a look he couldn't quite describe crossed Taya's face, then disappeared as quickly. She sipped her coffee. "My parents passed away within a year of each other. My two older sisters live out east. I've never married." Her voice hitched on the last word. "And I have no children. There's no one for Brando to attack."

A loner. Not surprising. "Ever come close? To marriage, I mean."

Her hesitation provided the answer. If he were to guess, she'd survived a painful breakup.

"Yes, but I'm grateful it didn't happen. The changes it would've required are more than I care to make at this stage of my life. Besides I've already given up too much. I've no desire to do that again, especially not for a man."

Ouch. A poignant response. "What'd you give up?"

She lingered again and glanced down. "A position within the FBI as a forensic anthropologist. I would have coheaded the department and lead criminal investigations in the Midwest."

"Sounds like a good career move."

"I suppose. But that's neither here nor there." Regret laced her reply.

"Would the position require you to also attend the FBI academy and qualify as an agent?" Failing the academy would explain her disdain for LEOs.

She snorted. "Absolutely not. I detest all things law enforcement related."

He sat up straighter. "Wow. Not sure what to do with that."

She shrugged. "Do whatever you'd like with it."

"Bad experience as a child?"

Taya leaned against the wall, crossing her arms. "I appreciate your interest in my history, however, I doubt my past benefits your contingency planning."

"Humor me."

She sighed. "I learned to loathe all things law enforcement when my ex-fiancé, Jeremy, betrayed me."

Protectiveness constricted Keegan's heart but that didn't explain her hatred of LEOs. "I don't mean to pry—"

"Thank you."

"But could you elaborate?"

She rolled her eyes. "Jeremy's an FBI agent and a born liar."

He blinked, trying to interpret her statement. "You think all law enforcement officers are liars?"

"Not all, but probably many. And adrenaline junkies."

Keegan laughed. "I wouldn't describe myself that way, but I guess there are some. I'm sorry Jeremy hurt you, but don't let one bad potato ruin the dinner."

Taya chuckled. "That's a unique approach on an old cliché."

"What did he do?"

"Left me for his FBI recruit partner."

"Got blindsided?"

She walked to the window and peered out. "Shouldn't have. Jeremy encouraged me to decline my FBI job offer. He didn't want us working for the same government agency because 'a couple needs separate interests,'" she said, using air quotes. "Translation, I intruded on his space and he worried I'd discover his infidelities with Gail. She's now his wife. They married a month after graduation." The hurt in her voice conveyed that the memories still stung.

Taya returned to the desk and sat down.

"Wow." Keegan took her hand. "An unappreciative loser who failed to see the wonderful things you bring to a relationship doesn't deserve your love. The best revenge is to be happy."

She yanked free and stood, crossing her arms. "Who said anything about revenge?" Before he responded, she asked, "What about you? Always wanted to join the ATF?"

If he didn't relent a little and share something personal, Taya might never open up. She'd earned a peek into his life and keeping details from her had lost its appeal. Keegan wanted to get to know Taya and it started with trusting her with his story.

"Yep. Applied right after college. Patrice followed in my footsteps after I convinced her she'd be a great asset to the DEA."

Her expression softened, and she sat again. "You loved her."

Strange comment. "Of course."

"How long were you a couple?" Taya looked down.

Keegan's head snapped up. "What? No. Patrice is my stepsister."

Taya's cheeks flushed a deep shade of red. "I just assumed—"

Did he detect relief? "My mom passed away when I was twelve. My dad married Patrice's mother, Ione, four years later." Keegan swallowed the unexpected boulder in his throat.

Taya gave his arm a gentle squeeze. "You grew up in a blended family. That couldn't have been easy."

Grateful for the redirection, he answered, "I loved Ione, but Patrice's gang involvement and drug use aged my father a decade their first year of marriage. Before she got herself arrested and thrown in jail, I had to do something. I saw the toll her antics had on our parents and jumped in."

"What did you do?" She sat beside him again.

"My pastor recommended mercy over judgment. I worked to build a relationship with her and eventually we got close. When she graduated college, I suggested she apply with the DEA. Her knowledge of drugs and gang affiliations made her a great asset to them."

"Was Patrice motivated?"

He chuckled. "Definitely. Adventurous. A spitfire. Patrice fit in like the position was custom-built for her. She moved up the ranks fast." He worked his hands around the empty soda bottle, regret filling his chest. "Her biggest weakness was making decisions. She came to me when the promotion opened and without realizing she'd work undercover, I encouraged her to go for it."

"What's wrong with wanting her to succeed?"

Success was fine, but he'd practically led Patrice to her death. The reminder brought on a fresh wave of guilt. "I set her up for failure."

Taya tilted her head and a long curl swept over her shoulder. "We don't know each other well, but I'm confident if the body at Ashfall is your stepsister, you are not responsible for her murder."

He couldn't respond. Was she correct in diagnosing he'd misplaced the blame? Ironically, the same way Taya blamed Jeremy's betrayal on LEOs? *Lord, blame weighs down a heart and blinds our eyes.*

"In my experience, most people aren't content with status quo."

He shrugged. "True. Brando's arrest would set me up for a great promotion in Missouri. That's my home state."

She slid off the desk, walked to the sleeping bag and busied herself rolling it up.

Keegan sensed an invisible wall had sprung up between them. What'd he do wrong? *Guess we're done talking about Dr. Taya McGill.*

He opted to revert to their earlier discussion. "This isn't the way I planned to spend the holidays. Back home, Ione makes a huge meal, and we open gifts after dinner. Then Patrice and I would have a not-so-friendly game of Scrabble, depending on who was winning." He withdrew Patrice's ring from his pocket. "It won't be the same without her."

Taya hugged the sleeping bag, then replaced it in the cabinet. "I'm truly sorry for your loss."

His phone chimed, interrupting them. Keegan pushed off the desk and glanced at the screen. "Bear, you here?"

"Yep, just pulled into town."

"I'll meet you by the back door." Keegan disconnected and faced Taya. "Stay here."

"No way. I'm going with you." She was at his side in an instant, determination etched in her expression.

He sighed. "Taya—"

"Are you worried Bear isn't safe?"

"Not in the least." The sound of an engine ended their standoff. "Fine, just let me lead."

"Got it."

They hurried down the stairs, Keegan's gun at the ready. Nearing the main floor, he paused and halted her with his hand, prepared for her argument. "Please wait here."

"What's the contingency plan?" Taya asked.

"We don't need one right now." Keegan walked away, her words ricocheting in his mind and the tiniest seed of doubt lingered. Wanda's text said Brando had postponed the meeting. Then he'd conceded to meet at dusk. Why the sudden change?

Taya's earlier question registered. If Brando discovered the connection between Keegan and Patrice, the meeting was a trap.

He paused, staring at the darkened hallway. A speck of concern settling between his shoulder blades. Taya needed a plan, because if Bear wasn't waiting outside the building, Keegan was a dead man.

With a groan, he spun on his heel and rushed to where Taya stood, concern written in her expression. He placed his phone in her hand. "If I'm not back in five minutes, get out of here and call Special Agent in Charge Otto Hawkins."

Taya's gaze remained transfixed on the hall where Keegan had disappeared.

He'd been wrong about the safe house and Earl. What if he was wrong about Bear, too?

A glance at her watch. He had one minute or she'd bolt from this fortress.

Serious but friendly tones echoed, accompanied by heavy footsteps.

Taya exhaled relief at Keegan's approaching familiar form. Pushing off the wall, she stood tall, studying the colossal man following him.

Keegan smiled. "Dr. Taya McGill, meet Bear Nichols."

The stranger stepped forward, hand outstretched, and his wide grin drew attention to his silver-and-white beard. The red Carhartt coat hugged his broad shoulders and muscular arms, and he wore dark jeans and black boots.

She extended her hand, which he enveloped between his. "Hello, Mr. Nichols."

"No mister anything. That's for old guys. Just Bear, ma'am." His voice rumbled like thunder.

She smiled. "Fair enough. Then no ma'am or doctor, please. Just Taya."

"Pleased to meet you."

"Likewise," Taya said, charmed by the gentle giant. She handed Keegan back his cell phone, which he pocketed.

"Let's head upstairs." Keegan motioned toward the steps.

Taya led the men to the third-floor classroom and they settled on the desktops.

"Bear's your official bodyguard while I'm gone. If you

need anything, let him know. I'll connect with him before I return here. Should something happen—" Keegan paused.

"Like what?" Taya asked, nervousness flooding her chest. The thought of being separated from him was suddenly unsettling.

Keegan continued, "Should you have to vacate the premises, Bear and I'll work out a meeting place."

"I'm not helpless. If something goes wrong, I need to know what our plan is." Irritation fueled her words.

"Pardon me, Taya," Bear began, his tone soft and steady with no allowance for discussion. "Please don't be offended by the lack of details. The man hunting you is clever and unpredictable at times. Keegan and I must remain fluid in our plan. It might require split-second decisions and changes. However, I'm at your disposal and here to serve you. I will do that to the utmost of my ability."

The man's proclamation deflated her angst, and something in his eyes poured reassurance over her heart. "Thank you, Mr. Nichols."

"I'll check in before returning here. I won't be gone long," Keegan inserted. "However, if I'm delayed, Bear will take you to my boss."

Taya understood. A lengthy meeting meant things weren't going well.

Keegan glanced at his watch. "I'd better scoot."

"We'll be finer than frog hair," Bear assured.

Keegan chuckled and slapped his friend on the shoulder. "Great." He faced Taya.

Bear pushed up from the desk. "I'll check out the building and see you out." He exited the room, leaving them alone.

Keegan walked to her and placed his hands on her shoulders, gazing into her eyes. "Taya, I'll see you soon and this will all be finished."

She wanted to agree, but barely managed a smile. Would

he hug her? Say something meaningful? The urge to ask him to stay had her biting her lip. She shook off the thought. No. She wasn't reliant upon any man.

"You're in good hands," he said, stepping back. Then, with one last glance over his shoulder, he left, footsteps fading.

Bear returned, carrying a large pistol.

She studied the man. Who was he? Another ATF agent? "Bear," Taya began. "I assume that's a nickname?"

He nodded. "Yep, wily as a bear." He winked and patted his robust stomach. "Don't let the size fool ya. I still got turbo in this old body."

She laughed despite the seriousness of the situation. "What do you do for a living?"

He swiped at his beard. "I'm retired. Now, I do a little of this and that. More that than this. Depends on the day."

"Quite the enigmatic statement."

He quirked a very overgrown eyebrow. "Beggin' your pardon?"

"Sorry, I only meant that doesn't answer the question."

He nodded. "Some questions aren't easily answered. I assure you, you're in good hands," he repeated Keegan's promise, then gestured toward the binoculars. "Mind if I look?"

"Please." She passed them and he peered out the window. "He's on his way to the Camp."

Taya moved closer. "Wait, in his SUV? They'll recognize it. Be able to run his plates and know his identity."

Bear laughed. "Nope, he's got my ride." He passed her the binoculars. "Have a look-see."

She spotted an old faded blue-and-white pickup. He drove toward an area with several single-level buildings, all painted an awful shade of green. The entrance sign read Camp 2963.

"I'm heading down. Gotta watch the perimeter. I understand you not wanting to be holed up in this room, but it's safer. Keep that door locked and don't open it for anyone."

"Not even you?" she quipped.

He chuckled. "Not even me. I'll open it with my lock pick. How about I give you a signal first?" He demonstrated with a clear whistle resembling a cardinal's song.

She nodded. "Sounds great."

"Good." He glanced down at the remaining kolaches. "May I?"

"Oh, yes, please. Forgive my bad manners."

"Raspberry, those are the best." He took a bite. "I'll check on ya in a jiffy."

Taya locked the door, then surveyed the classroom. Intricate handcrafted molding bordered the high ceiling. Chipped white paint—probably lead-based—covered the walls. Despite the aging architecture, the building was in good shape. A brick fortress as Keegan deemed it.

She stepped toward the window and touched the glass, leaving a dusty fingerprint. With Bear keeping watch, she had nothing to do but wait. Taya dropped to the floor and leaned against the wall, replaying her conversation with Keegan. She might have a disdain for law enforcement but she had to admit, Keegan wasn't like anyone she'd met before.

He'd eluded a criminal and driven them to safety. He'd introduced her to kolaches—a new favorite. She'd have to search for a bakery near her apartment in Lincoln.

Home. Alone. Not even a goldfish to welcome her. Taya sighed. She'd never minded before.

That was a lie. She'd learned to live in solitude, not expecting anything from anyone. No one to disappoint her. No one to leave her. Alone was always safer.

Except when Keegan spoke of his parents and Patrice with such fondness, Taya longed to experience that bond. She considered the sibling connection—one she'd never had with her sisters—that transcended blood relations with his family. Her heart wrenched at Keegan's vulnerability in sharing his perceived failures with his stepsister.

The more he talked, the more Taya wanted to know. *What? No.*

Their current situation wasn't the beginning of a relationship. Criminals threw them together, and they bonded in their combined efforts to seek justice for Patrice. Both just doing their jobs.

Taya enjoyed her career. With multiple duties, she'd seen much of Nebraska and worked unique cases, brought resolution for victims. And she'd taught anthropology students at the college. However, if the truth be known—a secret she wouldn't dare admit—she'd always bemoaned not joining the FBI. Her dream job.

Before Jeremy, she'd relished working side by side with law enforcement, solving mysteries and testifying with indisputable proof against the perpetrators who might've otherwise gotten away with their crimes. Helping people. It was a thrill beyond words.

A dream demolished by Jeremy and Gail's tidal wave of destruction.

She'd avoided the FBI and all things related to law enforcement as if doing so punished Jeremy. He didn't care. The only person harboring anger was her.

Taya pondered Keegan's advice. Maybe he was right, happiness was the best revenge. *I want joy in my life again.*

Keegan. Thinking of his handsome face and witty replies brought a warmth to her heart.

He made her feel alive.

Rehashing their conversation, she rushed to the window and peered out. What if Keegan didn't return? *Lord, please protect him.*

Taya walked to the desk and lifted the flashlight, then crossed the room and dropped to the floor, leaning against the wall. She was safe. Bear watched over her. She closed her eyes, replaying the conversation she and Keegan had shared. Thinking about him. Her muscles relaxed, and she inhaled deeply.

A thud jolted her into hypervigilance and her eyes flew open. How long had she napped? Every instinct beamed on high alert and she waited, listening for a repetition or subsequent noise. Something to either ease her fears or activate her body to flee.

Pulse in her ears, tormenting her with uncertainty, she sat immobile with her back against the wall, clutching Keegan's flashlight. Her gaze fixated on the door, praying the lock held. Where was the gun?

She scanned the area to the desk where the pistol sat on the opposite side of the room. Why hadn't she kept it beside her?

Taya got to her feet. Wary of making noise, she tiptoed to the door, verifying the brass lock remained in place. She released the breath she'd been holding, then crept to the desk and grabbed the gun. Cold and heavy in her hand, she took it with her to the window and peeked outside. She picked up the binoculars and surveyed the outdoors.

Nothing alarming.

No other clatter emitted.

You're safe. Bear would've returned if there was danger. She forced three invigorating breaths, then backed from the glass and put down the binoculars on the windowsill.

Night was encroaching and shadows stretched across the classroom floor, chasing away the precious remnants of daylight. Yet uneasiness hovered like the cobwebs decorating the pane, weaving worry through her rationalizations.

The gun weighed down her hand. She'd never shot any living creature, but if an intruder lurked beyond the protective walls, her survival depended on the weapon. She willed herself to be brave and crept to the door.

Determination fueling her, she placed both hands against the cool wood and listened.

Silence.

Then a growl, deep and throaty. Like a wounded animal.

Bear? He needed help!

His order not to leave the room argued with her compulsion to check on him.

She released the lock. The resonating click reverberated like a gong.

Taya lingered, then gripped the handle and tugged open the door, cringing at the ominous creak.

The rectangular windows diffused faint light onto the staircase, and the hallways on either side stretched into blackness. A resounding thud echoed, activating Taya's tightening grip on the gun.

She hadn't imagined the earlier noise.

Taya approached the banister, grasped hold of the splintered railing, then peered over. Her stomach lurched with vertigo, and a search of the inky darkness revealed no answers.

A shiver snaked down her back.

Taya jerked upright and looked over her shoulder.

Steady thuds below boomed like a grandfather clock, ticking away her fate.

Footsteps.

The pace increased. Not a run but hurried, fading, then intensifying.

The intruder searched.

For her.

Where was he? She couldn't rush down the stairs, he'd spot her.

Too risky.

The fire escape outside, accessible from a third-floor

classroom at the far end of the building. She searched the gloomy corridor.

But which room?

Taya skirted to the right, flipped on the flashlight and scoured the last room.

No opening.

She crossed the hall, entering the opposite classroom and spotted the escape chute door.

Boarded shut.

Desperation increased her courage. She turned off the flashlight and set it beside the gun on the windowsill. With both hands, she tugged at the wood.

The boards were unyielding.

Footsteps intensified, drawing closer.

Taya rushed to close and lock the door, then surveyed the space consumed by scattered desks and boxes. Opting to hide behind a cabinet, she squatted and peered around it, maintaining visual of the door.

She reached for the gun, but grazed something soft instead.

A dead mouse.

Taya sucked in her scream and shuddered in disgust.

Where was the weapon?

Foreboding slammed into her. She'd left it by the chute opening. *No. Oh, no.* Dread and fear swirled, tightening her stomach.

Did she have time to retrieve it?

The doorknob rattled.

Too late!

Heart jackhammering, she wiped her palms on her pants. Took a deep breath.

He made another attempt, then walked away.

Had he given up and gone downstairs? Or was he waiting for her to exit the room?

She counted to twenty and, hearing no other sounds,

rushed to the chute. Snatching the flashlight and gun, she crept toward the door and pressed her ear against the wood.

Nothing.

Please, Lord, let him be on another floor. Help me escape.

She eased the lock. Finally, it clicked.

Taya sucked in a breath, then tugged open the door and peered into the vacated hallway before exiting the room.

Muted sounds reached her. Which floor was he on?

She couldn't hide forever. The stairs were risky but there was no other option short of leaping from a window. In a rapid tiptoe, she scurried down, taking two and three steps at a time.

Footfalls echoed below.

Taya lunged into a classroom on the second floor and reached to close the door.

No knob. She pushed the door closed, and it creaked in revolt.

Fast ascent from the stairs.

He'd heard her.

She spun, but the empty room provided no hiding places, and boards covered every window.

Trapped!

Taya backed against the farthest wall and hefted the gun, aiming at the door. Her hands shook with adrenaline and she fought to stabilize the weapon.

She held her breath, willing herself to remain silent.

Please go. Please go.

A tickle on her neck sent her frigid. A spider? She squeezed her eyes shut, frantic to swipe it away, but dared not move.

Taya strained to gauge his location over her heart's drumming.

Had he gone the other way? She'd have time to make it down the stairs.

She rushed to the door and yanked it open.

"Dr. McGill, I'm so glad you're okay." Officer Folze eclipsed the doorway, preventing her escape.

Taya skidded to a stop, gasping and stumbled backward.

He took a step toward her. Sweat dripped down his jowls. "I've been searching all over this wretched place for you."

"Where's Bear?" Taya insisted, hoisting the gun higher.

Folze tilted his head, resembling a confused basset hound. "Bear, ma'am?"

"Yes, where is he?" She searched his face for signs of deceit.

"Dr. McGill, I'm sorry I don't know who that is. But you're safe with me. You can put down that gun."

Her hands shook. "How'd you find me here?"

"We have to leave before that bad man returns," Folze insisted, stepping closer.

"What bad man?"

"The kidnapper at Ashfall."

Keegan had been undercover, so of course Folze thought he was a criminal. Except… "You saw him?"

Folze blinked and stepped closer. "I'll explain everything, but we have to get out of here."

The same argument Keegan made at Ashfall when they'd first met. But the warning flags waving in her brain said this was a very different situation. Taya held up her hands. "Stop!"

He halted, and she redirected, "Why weren't you guarding the remains at Ashfall? Did you see who took them?"

"When I saw your ransacked motor home…" He swallowed. "I'm not proud, ma'am, but I panicked and ran."

"Did you notify the police?"

"I couldn't. I'd lose my job." He exhaled with exaggerated emphasis. "You don't understand the men you're up against. We need to leave. Now."

The illogical explanation intensified her flight instincts.

He shuffled from one cowboy boot to another, nervous. She had to get away. Fast. He'd never catch her if she ran.

Except he blocked the doorway. "Please put down the gun. I'm an officer. I won't hurt you."

Taya took a slow grapevine step to the side, remaining out of his reach, pistol trained on his chest.

Folze rubbed his beefy hand over his stubble-covered chin. "All right, Dr. McGill, truth is I haven't been completely honest with you."

"Oh?"

"I know where the bones are. I'll show you."

Taya hesitated.

Folze's jaw tightened, impatience edging his tone. "Ma'am, I don't want to force you."

Comical, considering she held the gun, but bluffing cooperation might work better.

"Okay." She lowered the weapon, maintaining her hold, and approached him with confidence.

When she was inches from him, Folze clamped a hand on her left arm, attempting to stop her.

She spun and slammed the butt of the gun into his nose.

Stunned, he cried out, releasing her. His hands flew to his nose to stop the bleeding.

She lunged through the door. But Folze's long reach caught her ankle, lifting her airborne. She dropped face-first on the floor.

Taya rolled onto her back and tried to squeeze the trigger. It didn't budge. She squeezed harder.

Folze laughed, crimson smears on his face. "You forgot the safety."

She scooted to her feet. Not fast enough. He pounced, tackling her and beat the weapon from her hand.

Taya clawed at him, and her finger caught on something, yanking it free. A distance *ting*. Whatever it was bounced on the wood. But she didn't stop. Arms flailing, legs kicking. He leaned closer and Taya dug her fingers into his eyes.

He screamed, falling backward.

Taya jumped to her feet and sprinted down the hall.

"Dr. McGill!" His footsteps thundered behind her.

Taya pumped her arms, pushing until at last she gripped the handrail, rounding the corner and caught sight of Folze. Too close.

She descended the stairs, struggling to avoid the broken steps.

"Stop!" he heaved.

Taya tripped, and her foot broke through the splintered wood. Pain radiated up her leg. She tugged, freeing her trapped appendage, and spotted a yellow blur in her peripheral.

Folze aimed a Taser.

She shrieked. Her muscles spasmed in one solid contraction. Agony tentacled through her body. Unable to stop the motion, Taya lost her balance and fell backward. Her gaze focused on the intricately carved ceiling just before everything went black.

EIGHT

"Get out of here," Wanda screeched. Fear flickered in her bloodshot eyes, and she nibbled on a fingernail.

Keegan clenched the steering wheel, exuding a patience he didn't feel. Between her tears and shrill tone, he couldn't understand a word she said. "Calm down, and tell me what's going on."

The Camp sat a mile up the road, atop the hill, and dusk was morphing into night. Wanda had flagged him down on the side of the road behind a grove of trees, frantic and jumpy as a Chihuahua after drinking a bucket of espresso. Bear's pickup rumbled, urging Keegan to get going, and his frustration neared boiling temperatures.

Wanda sucked in a breath and spewed in one long staccato sentence, "Brando's men want revenge, and they're calling you a traitor. Rumor is you took out Skull."

"Where'd you hear that?" Not a denial, not affirmation. The accusation might work to his benefit with Brando.

She shrugged and stepped back, antsy. Shoving her hands into her pockets, Wanda swayed from side to side, still rambling, "Dunno. But they're waiting for you. Brando knows you're coming."

Keegan calmed his voice. She must be tweaking. "I know. I'm meeting with Brando, remember?"

"No!" Wanda slapped both hands on the driver's door

and leaned in, eyes darting nervously. "Go. They're gonna kill you!"

"I'm late. We'll talk later." He reached for the gearshift.

She scrubbed a hand down her face. "Brando knows who you really are, *Agent* Stryker."

The emphasis on his title drove a shiver up Keegan's back. He studied Wanda. Was it true? The woman's eccentric and dramatic behavior wasn't uncommon, and to his knowledge, she'd never lied to him. All of the buildup and excitement of believing this meeting was the beginning of the end evaporated. Once he crested the hill to the Camp, would Brando's men ambush him?

"How do you know this?"

She backed away, shaking her head. "You gotta go."

He twisted around, spotting only the tip of the school's roof in the distance. Taya was with safe with Bear. Wasn't she?

Fear punched him in the gut with the force of a bomb. Did Brando's men know where Taya and Bear hid? Urgency coursed through his veins. He had to get back to Taya.

"Now!" Wanda urged. "They're coming!" She sprinted into the grove of trees.

"Wanda!"

She ignored Keegan, disappearing in the foliage.

The growl of an engine drew his attention. Furious, he eyed the familiar blue dually barreling for him. Earl.

Keegan shifted into Reverse, then yanked the wheel and turned the truck. The shift sent his cell phone flying off the seat and onto the floorboards. No time to retrieve it. He accelerated in the opposite direction. He'd lose Earl, then call Bear.

But a speeding sedan centered ahead of him, requiring a new plan. They had him trapped.

Keegan jerked the wheel to the right and drove through a neighboring pasture.

Had the pursuers seen him talking to Wanda? She'd risked her life to warn him. Why hadn't she called or texted rather than waiting for him there?

A dirt road loomed ahead. Both Earl and the sedan continued to follow, but the car fell behind, struggling to traverse the rough terrain. Earl's dually advanced.

He had to get back to the school, but he wouldn't lead Brando's cronies there. He'd have to lose them first.

He barreled through a ditch, and the pickup fishtailed on the soft shoulder before lurching back onto the road. The car attempted to do the same, but got stuck on the decline.

Mission accomplished.

Earl mimicked Keegan's move, deep in pursuit. *Scratch that.*

He'd lose the dually in heavier traffic.

Keegan accelerated away from Brunswick and at the Y intersection turned onto a paved county road, staying ahead of Earl—not by much—on the mile-long drive.

Keegan merged onto Highway 20 between a semi and a cattle hauler. Earl zoomed into the oncoming lane, almost colliding with another vehicle and cut off the semi. A blare of the truck's horn and flashing headlights confirmed the move wasn't appreciated.

The hauler neared another hill and prevented Keegan from passing. Earl kept pace and the semi lined up behind his dually.

They were boxed between the two large trucks. Perfect.

A building labeled Oakton Farm Supply sat on the left side of the road. No other vehicles approached from the westbound lanes. Keegan sped up as if to pass the cattle hauler, then at the last second, took a hard left into the company's parking lot. Earl whipped by, stuck between the cattle hauler and the semi, and Keegan grinned with satisfaction.

Snatching his cell phone from the floorboards, Keegan

dialed Bear's number. The line rang, then went to voice mail. Fear etched his heart. He never should've left Taya. He shifted and reversed direction, merging back onto Highway 20 in the westbound lane and headed for the school. His pulse raged and urgency propelled him.

Please, Lord, keep Taya and Bear safe.

Keegan couldn't shake the suspicion a mole existed in the ATF. Or had someone overheard his conversation with Hawk?

Bear's commitment to protect Taya was the only assurance Keegan clung to, but doubt plagued him. Brando's cronies possessed an indisputable ability of keeping one step ahead of him all the time. The idea that he'd never again see Taya soured his stomach. He hated traversing that mental road, however, strategic planning and acceptance of the inevitable required consideration of every possible scenario.

Was Taya okay? Bear would've called if they'd encountered issues. Unless…

Hopelessness beckoned, but Keegan refused to surrender. He'd entrusted Taya to the most qualified man he'd ever known. Bear's extensive military and civilian careers made him a force to be reckoned with and they were safe at the schoolhouse. He could fight off an army by himself. Besides, the distance alone provided Bear and Taya a head start should they be forced to flee. Unless Brando's men had come from another direction and surrounded them.

Please, Lord, help me get there in time.

Brando had discovered Keegan's identity. How? The pictures and message must've sent from Skull's phone. This case was filled with too many annoying questions, all of which would piece together the mystery behind Patrice's murder.

Keegan hit redial. Bear's voice mail answered. He shoved the phone into his pocket, anxiety increasing. Pedal to the floor, he pushed the old pickup as fast as he could safely drive across the country roads.

Each passing second felt more like hours. *Please, Lord, let Taya be alive.*

At last the school loomed ahead. Keegan spotted his SUV with four flat tires parked on the backside of the brick building. He slammed into Park and threw open the door, leaping from the truck. Using the flashlight app on his cell, he scanned the entrance and spotted a small silver tranquilizer dart.

No.

Keegan bolted through a side door into the dark building, sweeping the light through the hallway.

"Bear? Taya?" His cry reverberated off the empty walls.

A chill slithered down his back. He rushed to the foyer, and his foot collided with something soft, tripping him. Keegan stumbled into the wall to keep from falling, then turned and inspected the large form.

Bear. A half-eaten raspberry kolache lay near his hand. A second tranquilizer dart near his neck.

Keegan dropped to his knees and shook his friend. "Bear! Wake up."

No response from the man's placid body.

"Please don't be dead." Keegan leaned closer.

Bear exhaled shallow breaths and his skin was cold and clammy. A bluish hue tainted his lips. Using his fingertips, Keegan gently pried open Bear's eyelids. The pupils were tiny, the size of a pin tip. All the signs of fentanyl poisoning.

The abundance of opioid drug overdoses motivated law enforcement to provide the antidote—Narcan—to every officer. Keegan was grateful he'd hidden two bottles on his person at all times since he'd first infiltrated Brando's group. Couldn't be too careful when the job required daily interaction with addicts.

He tugged off his motorcycle boot and dug out the bottle of Narcan, then using his teeth, ripped open the package. Inserting the bottle tip into Bear's nostrils, Keegan deployed the medicine and his gaze landed on the stairs.

Bear sucked in a breath and groaned, slowly coming to.

"Thank God!" Keegan jumped to his feet and dialed 9-1-1.

"Operator, what's your—"

"Need an ambulance to the Brunswick abandoned school. Victim is male. Fifty-six-years old. Bertrand Nichols. He's retired LEO. Tranquilizer darts and possible fentanyl exposure."

"Sir—"

"Narcan deployed." Keegan disconnected, not giving the operator time to quiz him, and using his phone's flashlight, ran up the first flight of stairs, then paused near the second-floor landing. A large hole gaped from one step, a smear and several droplets on the next stair. Blood.

Fury raged through him on the heels of worry. He sprinted to the second floor and surveyed the area.

Keegan spotted the gun he'd given to Taya. He rushed to inspect it. The safety was still locked. His stomach tightened. Had she forgotten to release it? Had he failed to remind her it was on? He'd assumed she knew how to fire a weapon.

Recalling their first interaction, she'd clearly said she didn't own any guns. He threw back his head, staring at the ceiling. He should've confirmed she was comfortable using the weapon. At the very least, gone over the basics with her. Taya used intellectualism as her method of self-protection. She'd never confess lack of knowledge or skill because she'd see it as a weakness. But he should've known better.

He'd blown it and set her up to fail. Despair covered him, and he tucked the gun into his waistband. Turning, a glimmer caught his attention. A small brass button. He snatched the button and studied the embossed pine trees.

Loud hacking coughs drew him back to where Bear lay on his side.

Keegan raced down the stairs. "Where's Taya?"

Bear heaved and pointed to the tranquilizer dart. "Drugged."

He helped Bear to sit up and squatted beside him. "Did you see who took Taya? What happened?"

Bear shook his head, the coughs subsiding. "What? She's gone. No!" He released a guttural growl. "It all happened so fast. I heard something and came down to investigate." He inhaled. "When I stepped out the door, something stuck me in the back of the neck. I ripped out a tranquilizer dart—"

"I know, I saw it outside," Keegan interrupted.

"Right." Bear sucked in another breath. "Came back in and started up the stairs to get Taya. I felt woozy, stumbled and got another pinch in my neck. The creep shot me again! I yanked out the dart, but the tranquilizer was already working. I tried to get to her. Whatever he used took me out. I fell and he rushed at me, blew some sort of dust in my face. I gasped and everything went black."

"He must've mixed the fentanyl with a powder. That might be why you survived. If you were already knocked out, you wouldn't inhale as deeply."

"What fentanyl?"

Keegan gave him a quick update on his condition upon arrival. "Did you see the guy who shot you?"

"Nah, he had something covering his face. Big guy, though."

Keegan lifted the dart from the floor and inspected it. "Two of these would take down a bear." He grimaced.

Bear grunted. "Yeah, I know."

"I found this upstairs." He showed Bear the button.

"Gimme some light."

Keegan held up his phone, allowing him to study the button. Time was slipping away and he needed to hurry but without a lead—

"It's a uniform—"

"Game and parks! Folze!" Keegan punched the floor. "Ugh! How did he find you guys?"

Bear didn't hesitate. "Your phone."

"This is the cell I used to contact my team. He wouldn't—" Keegan stood and paced. "Wanda warned me that Brando knows my real identity."

"And you think there's a mole in the system."

"Exactly! Anyone with access to my contact information would have the number and be able to trace it."

"What else?"

"The only person besides you who knows about this place is Hawk." Keegan ran a hand over his neck.

Bear reached into his pocket and removed his phone. "Take mine and leave yours here."

Keegan made the trade and continued pacing. "Where would he take her?"

"What do you know about him?" Even after recovering from two tranquilizer darts and what could've been a deadly poisoning, Bear's tactical brain went into action.

"If he's working for Brando—" Were they at the Camp? No, Keegan would have seen Folze driving up the road when Brando's men ambushed him. "Taya said he's lazy."

"Start with his home address."

"He's not that dumb," Keegan argued.

Bear snorted and the action brought on a new round of hacking coughs. "Criminals are stupid. He'll go somewhere he's comfortable. Get inside his head."

"Right." Keegan searched the internet using Bear's phone and discovered a listing for G. Folze. "He's got a place in Orchard, about fifteen miles away."

"Start there."

"I need your pickup."

Sirens screamed in the distance.

Bear waved an enormous hand. "Get outta here before they ask questions."

Any other time, Keegan would've demanded a manhunt for the criminal, but Brando's far-reaching connections left him questioning. And he was already wanted for Skull's murder.

"Go!" Bear commanded.

"One more thing. Find my CI, Wanda Vicory. She's in danger if Brando discovers she warned me."

"I'll take care of it. Now go!"

"I'll be in touch." Keegan bolted from the building and jumped into Bear's still-running pickup.

Blue-and-red lights strobed behind him.

Pedal to the floor, mind racing out of control, he headed east toward the town of Orchard, praying the entire way. He'd been wrong about so many things. He couldn't afford to be wrong about this.

Taya strained to open her eyes against the college drumline battling inside her head, threatening nausea. Her back and arms ached from the hard surface swaying beneath her.

Her restricted movement was combined with the burning sensation of something digging into her skin.

He'd bound her hands behind her.

She inhaled the stench of glue and blinked. Panic rising, she exhaled a muffled cry for help into the tape covering her mouth.

Short, anxious breaths through her nose made it hard to breathe. Logic warned she had to regain her composure before she passed out again.

Breathe, Taya! Where was she? They were moving. In a car? No, a truck. Tires bounced through ruts, slamming her body against the unforgiving floorboard. A new blast of pain coursed through her head. The force acted like a reset button, and Taya attempted some controlled breathing techniques to even out her heart rate and process her surroundings.

The deep rumble of the engine indicated she was in a big truck—crew cab, based on her location in the back. She stared at the dark gray ceiling. A soft glow emitted from the dashboard, and the window conveyed it was nighttime. How long had she been unconscious?

Taya lifted her head, spotting a pouch on the seat above as well as the source of the rattling near her feet. A toolbox. She'd find a weapon in there and a way to remove her bindings. First, she had to reverse her position without drawing the driver's attention—Folze, no doubt—before they reached their destination. Where was he taking her?

Think. The nightmare memories played, and she recalled running from Folze. Her foot crashing through the step, and the cataclysmic mistake of looking behind her. Her stomach tightened as she remembered Folze shooting her with his Taser. The voltage had forced her into a conscious immobilized state. She'd fallen backward and must've smacked her head on the wood, knocking her out.

Oh, Lord. What do I do now? Tears threatened but Taya refused to allow them to fall, returning instead to the familiarity of anger. How dare that wretched mess of a man attack her! She'd misjudged Folze's slothfulness, assuming he was a wimp. The idea that the officer could be a criminal hadn't registered as a possibility.

She'd underestimated his abilities.

And he'd underestimated her fortitude.

Keegan's assurances that Bear would protect her had lessened her guard. She'd trusted them both. How had Folze gotten past Bear? He'd seemed confused and disinterested when she'd asked about him. He could've faked the response. What if Folze and Bear were working together?

Keegan hadn't hesitated, adamant about trusting his friend, and she'd relied on his word. Now, she wasn't sure what to believe about anyone.

Had Folze hurt Bear? If he'd used the Taser or gunned the man down... She'd not imagined the cry, and instinct told her it'd come from Bear. Taya swallowed hard. If a man as skilled and immense as he was hurt or worse, what hope did she have of surviving Folze?

Where was Keegan? He'd gone alone, without backup. Without contacting his superiors. If he was hurt...or...

No. She wouldn't go down that dead-end road because Keegan was her last hope of rescue. He had to be okay and he had to find her.

What if he didn't?

She'd dodged death too many times since arriving at Ashfall. Maybe her number was up.

The pendulum of emotions simulated the vehicle's movement, dragging her into sadness. Like Patrice's death, it might take months or years for anyone to find her body. Worse, who would care?

The solitude she'd established gave her independence from needy relationships, protecting her heart. Reliant on no one else, she'd escaped disappointment. She'd taken care of herself since Jeremy's betrayal. She wouldn't let another uniformed bully steal what she'd fought to regain, her self-confidence and future. Her survival meant she couldn't lie here waiting for Folze to kill her.

A renewed boldness motivated Taya to fight against the restraints, to no avail. However, her legs weren't bound. She tilted her head, spotting the door handle. She'd push herself to a sitting position and...what? Without the use of her hands, how would she open the door?

"Say your command," a robotic voice said, indicating Folze had used a hands-free device.

Taya froze.

"Call Brando," Folze replied.

"Calling Brando," the electronic voice responded.

Loud ringing boomed over the speakers.

"What," a woman answered.

"Get me Brando," Folze replied.

"He ain't around."

"Yes, he is. And he's waiting for my call," Folze insisted. "He's gonna want to hear what I have to say."

Muffled voices.

Fear coursed through Taya.

"What do you want, Folze?" a man asked, his tone annoyed.

"Brando, I took care of it."

Taya blinked. Took care of what?

"Congratulations. You finally did something right."

"Want me to finish off the doc?"

Taya swallowed.

"No, Vice will handle her," Brando said.

Who was Vice? *Lord, help me.*

"I found something but since I've gone above and beyond my assignment, I need a bigger payout."

"Don't play games with me. I'll kill you myself."

"Oh, it's very interesting footage. Patrice Nunes was a busy girl," Folze blurted.

Taya held her breath. He'd found the SIM card. Anger at the backstabbing, two-faced excuse of an officer had her gritting her teeth. She had to escape before Folze handed her over to Brando.

A pause, then Brando said, "You've got three seconds."

"The video implicates one of your people. So, let's talk money first," Folze negotiated, arrogance in his tone.

"What do you want?"

"Double our agreed price."

"Are you out of your mind?" Brando raged over the speakers.

"I'll be at my cabin." Folze disconnected. "Yes!" He turned on the radio and bellowed out of tune with a country remake of a familiar Christmas song.

Taya exhaled surrender, her arms ached from the restraints. She squeezed her eyes shut. *Lord, I can't do this alone. I need Your help.*

Even if Keegan searched for her, how would he find her? Once Folze handed over the SIM card, Keegan's cover would be blown. If he wasn't already dead, he would be soon. The anger she'd held only moments before evaporated.

Keegan didn't deserve to die. Everything she hated about the badge didn't apply to the kind man. He'd listened to her. Worked beside her to try to find the SIM card, always treating her as an equal. Unlike Jeremy, who'd made her feel stupid and inadequate every day of their time together.

Her eyes burned with tears. Taya blinked them back out of sheer rebellion. Crying was a weakness she couldn't afford.

Patrice Nunes deserved justice, and Keegan was the one to make that happen.

Taya eased to a partial sitting position—grateful for every ab crunch of her daily exercise routine—and swiveled on her behind, fingers searching for the toolbox lid. Locked!

The truck slowed and gravel crunched beneath the tires. Taya reassessed her situation. If Folze thought her unconscious, he wouldn't be prepared for an attack or her escape. She returned to her original position.

The truck stopped and Folze shut off the engine. That

meant they weren't going anywhere fast. He planned to be here for a length of time.

He opened the door and got out, shutting the door.

Taya closed her eyes and steadied her breathing. With her arms bound, she couldn't fight him, but once he pulled her from the vehicle, she'd run with everything she had.

The back door opened and strong arms hoisted her out by her shoulders. Blood rushed to her head and pressure against her stomach conveyed that Folze had her in a fireman's carry. She opened one eye, careful not to draw attention. She was facing his back, damp with perspiration.

"I should get extra for all this work," Folze mumbled.

Taya surveyed the run-down ranch house and several Quonset buildings, all decrepit and scary. But Folze moved away from the structures, aiming for a grove of trees.

Taya's mind spun. She'd have to get back to the truck and drive away. Who knew how far they were from civilization? With her hands bound, she'd struggle to outrun Folze and without a doubt that Taser would stop her if he got too close. She had to get to the truck or inside the house. As soon as he set her down, she'd make a run for it.

He huffed and slowed in front of a door with chipped paint. Embedded in the ground, it resembled a coffin.

A root cellar.

Folze shifted her, and she forced her facial muscles to relax, eyes closed. Better he thought her unconscious. He set her down on her right side against the icy ground and turned his back to work the lock. Hands bound behind her back, Taya had to wriggle to her knees. She pushed up, getting to her feet. Once upright, she ran, battling the loss of her equilibrium and limping against the intense pain in her ankle.

No time to whine, but the injury compromised her speed.

She ran as fast as her legs would carry her, aiming for the trees.

"Hey!"

She didn't dare turn around as she dodged between the foliage.

"Come back here now!"

The truck loomed just a few feet ahead.

A *pop* sounded behind her.

Taya screamed but the tape muffled the cry.

Without her hands, she couldn't open the truck door, much less drive away. She'd run for the road. Maybe someone would stop and help her.

She took off, feet pounding the cold ground.

"Dr. McGill, you're making this harder than it has to be."

Taya reached a round wood rail fence with logs two feet apart. Too high to jump, too low to crawl under with bound hands. She ducked to squeeze between the logs and got her first leg through, just as a pinch impaled her side.

The hesitation provided Folze the chance to catch up. He yanked her backward, and her chin whacked against a log.

The world grew fuzzy but Taya fought to maintain consciousness. If she passed out, it would be over. He dragged her closer.

She wriggled, screamed and kicked, but Folze was stronger. He bound her ankles with plastic zip ties, then hoisted her over his shoulder. His arms tightened on her legs.

He hauled her back to the root cellar, and she watched in horror as he unlocked the door. The drugs coursed through her system, blurring her vision.

Folze lifted her and descended into the abyss. He flopped Taya onto the cold, hard earth.

She looked up. Three Folzes swayed before her.

Once he closed those doors, she'd be enveloped in darkness. But her body wouldn't move.

He laughed and secured her ankles and wrists to a shelf in the cellar. "Nighty night."

He ascended the stairs, each footstep more foreboding and terrifying than the last.

Please, don't do this. Taya whimpered against the tape over her mouth.

The door slammed shut above, engulfing her in the musty cavern black as pitch.

Were her eyes open or closed? She couldn't tell.

Taya shivered, battling to stay conscious, but cold spread through her body and dug deep into her bones. She returned to the place where her imagination had flown freely to Keegan. She focused on his strong jaw and soulful eyes.

Lord, please be with him, wherever he is. Please let him be okay.

A thud outside. She twitched. The tranquilizer made its way through her system, reminding her of the thick liquid inside a lava lamp. The room rocked and her eyes grew heavy.

Please. One word.

A prayer.

A plea.

An apology.

NINE

Frantic to find Taya, Keegan was crawling out of his skin by the time he reached Orchard. His unending prayers for her protection, combined with gratitude for finding Bear in time, were countered with his nonstop pondering of the evidence.

Sadness and fury warred within him. He'd failed her.

Just like Patrice.

No. There would be plenty of time for self-loathing after he found Taya—alive. Whatever it cost, he'd make sure her life didn't end the way Patrice's had. He wouldn't lose another woman he cared about.

Taya had grown on him in a way he hadn't expected. Her intelligence combined with a sweet naivete was refreshing. Not that he'd pursue her, or that she'd want anything more than friendship with him.

How many times had he heard women didn't want the uncertainty of their spouse coming home safely every night? He'd made the choice a long time ago to devote his life to the ATF and shied from relationships.

But Keegan reasoned that romance wasn't what intrigued him about Taya. It was the duty to demonstrate all LEOs men weren't like her dirtbag ex, Jeremy.

Although Folze's kidnapping reinforced her beliefs about backstabbing cops.

Keegan had to restore her faith in law enforcement and prove that cowards like Folze and Jeremy weren't the norm, but the exception. Redirecting his energy, he evaluated the facts.

Brando had lured Keegan away from the schoolhouse with the agreement to meet at the Camp, counting on his cronies to kill Keegan. He faced an army. One man against Brando's mob made for impossible odds. But if his team was compromised, he'd be on his own anyway. Unable to reconcile whether it was safe to contact Hawk, Keegan held off.

He'd continue the mission alone.

For now.

His internal vows carried him the remaining distance. Folze's home was located at the end of a dirt road on the corner of an immense cornfield. He approached slowly, turning off his headlight, and prepared for reconnaissance. Double-checking the address, Keegan confirmed he was in the correct—albeit rundown—place and parked behind the shelterbelt of trees on the north side.

With one last survey, he grabbed a flashlight from the console, slid from behind the wheel and crept around the pickup. No interior lights glowed from the house, and no vehicles were parked outside.

He stepped back, eyeing the dingy chipped siding in desperate need of replacement. The single garage door was missing, covered by wooden boards in varying shades of stain. Dead, overgrown weeds surrounded the walkway and climbed up the structure where missing shingles and haphazard storm drains gave the home a deserted appearance.

Keegan started with the closest of the three Quonset buildings.

Gun in hand, he made his way toward the metal structure, using shadows as cover. Frigid temperatures maintained remnants of packed down snow. Tire tracks led to the house and the dirt road peeked through sparse melted patches, indicating Folze had returned here sometime after the last snowstorm.

Keegan cleared the first two buildings—vacant minus aged farm equipment, blocks of hay, and a herd of feral cats—but a large padlock prevented entrance to the last. He located a crowbar in the second building and broke off the lock, hope building.

Taya had to be inside.

Scratch that. The locked Quonset held a pristine, fire-engine-red sports car. An unusual possession, considering Folze's dump of a house.

Keegan located a vehicle registration card inside the glove box, complete with a South Dakota address. *Please let Taya be there.*

He shoved the registration into his pocket and walked out of the Quonset. Relieved Brando's army wasn't waiting to attack him, he couldn't shake his frustration at Folze and Taya's absence. Was he overlooking something? Was she being held prisoner in the house?

Quiet echoed over the miles of surrounding cornfields— devoid of barking dogs, passing vehicles and the villainous game and parks officer—and the cold wind whistled against his ears. He sized up the ranch, surrounded by towering trees with sparse branches peeking in every direction—creating privacy and adding to the creepiness.

Dirty and neglected, it was evident Folze didn't care about this place. So why leave his sports car here?

Keegan crossed to the house and attempted to peer inside. Broken blinds covered the window and the front door was locked. He followed the cracked cement path, with varying degrees of vegetation sprouting through, and caught a glimpse of a partial footprint.

Pace quickening, he tromped over the snow-packed

ground. His grip tightened around the weapon, and he trained it on the ajar back door.

He entered the kitchen. Fast-food wrappers were scattered over the table, floor and counter. A stack of dishes consumed the sink. Open drawers and cabinets completed the disaster, indicating an obvious search. Had Brando's men beat him here? Did they have Taya?

Keegan continued clearing the home, anxiety ratcheting up with each step.

Folze didn't lack for junk. Clothes and shoes lay all over the living room floor and knickknacks filled the small bookshelf containing everything except books. A bulletin board covered with pictures of a cabin and the same red sports car hung over an old desk.

He studied the newer build of the house in the photo, a beautiful riverfront log cabin. Idyllic and serene. Some place Folze dreamed about going, or did he own it?

He ripped off the cabin photo, noting the immense cement bridge in the distance and familiar landmark sign. Chief Standing Bear Bridge crossed the Missouri River, connecting Nebraska and South Dakota. It was an easy commute back and forth across the river, so it wasn't inconceivable that Folze owned a cabin there. And locals joked the taxes were cheaper in South Dakota.

Taxes! He glanced again at the picture. Maybe Folze had left a paper trail.

Keegan rummaged through the mess in the desk.

Nothing.

"Come on!" He kicked the drawer and it rolled over, revealing a pink scrap taped underneath with three sets of double digits written in a scrawl. A safe combination code?

Keegan pocketed the paper and searched the house for anything resembling a safe or lockbox but found nothing. Discouraged, he exited the house, heading toward the pickup.

Muted clanging halted him. He swept the light over the ground, spotting a small smoke stack peeking from a snow drift and a door with white chipped paint.

A root cellar. Not uncommon for homes in the area.

He glanced around again. Would Folze have left Taya here? Unattended? The hair rose on his neck and he turned on his heel.

Not a sound. Yet instinct told him something was wrong. Very wrong.

Keegan rushed toward the door, slipping on the icy ground, hope increasing with each step. The snow hadn't melted naturally with the other patchy areas. Rather, it had been cleared off, exposing the aging brick, rock and cement blocks beneath. Long-rotted wood planks gave the door frame the appearance of a coffin. A shiver coursed through him, adding fuel to his suspicions that the cavelike prison held Taya. A latch and a second padlock. But his gaze froze at the rust-colored splotches.

Blood.

A second muffled thud emitted from below.

"Taya!"

Taya lay on her side tugging against the restraints where Folze had bound her to one of the cellar's wooden shelf legs. The structure rocked slightly, encouraging her to pull harder.

She yanked with all her might, and the heavy planks rained down on her. Unable to shield her face, she closed her eyes and waited for the wooden shower to stop.

With a slam, the last plank landed, and her wrists broke loose from the shelf but remained bound. Folze had put two sets of zip ties around her wrists and ankles and both remained tight against her skin. Wriggling into a sitting position, she focused on her memory of the cellar layout. She had to get to the stairs.

Scratching and pounding above from the cellar door froze her in place.

Help or Folze returning to kill her?

"Taya?"

Was she losing her mind? *Keegan?*

A creak above wafted in cold fresh air, but everything remained dark.

Taya's plea for help stuck in the tape.

A light appeared, moving toward her. She blinked against the sudden brightness, desperate to make out the form descending.

Keegan. Her eyes blurred with tears.

He skidded to her side, pulling her into his arms. "Thank God, you're alive!"

"You came for me," she attempted to say, but the mumbled garble made no sense to her own ears.

"What?" He leaned back and winced. "No wonder you didn't answer me. Hang on, this is gonna burn."

She braced, and he ripped off the tape. Her mouth and cheeks stung, and she sucked in a breath, filling her lungs.

"I don't know if Folze will return. Let's get out of here and then we'll talk." He gently brushed her hair from her face.

"He bound my ankles and wrists to the shelves. I pulled them down, but the zip ties didn't break." She jerked her chin in the direction of the heap of wood.

Keegan examined the restraints. "So that was the crash I heard. Brilliant! I'll carry you out and then we'll remove them. I don't know how much time we have."

"Okay."

He turned off the flashlight and tucked his gun into his waistband. Of course, he couldn't carry the light, the gun and her.

He lifted and cradled her against his powerful chest. She

inhaled the mingling scents of wood, earth and his leather jacket. He stood and walked toward the stairs.

"Thank you, Agent Stryker, for being as predictable as Brando said you'd be."

Keegan paused, and Taya turned toward the voice, though she didn't need to see the man's face to know who'd spoken.

Folze eclipsed the door. Gun aimed at them.

This nightmare never ended.

"Get out of my way," Keegan growled.

They were trapped.

Keegan's hold on her meant he couldn't reach his gun. And her bindings prevented her from helping.

Folze guffawed. "A shame you both have to die." The threat hung thick with intent, and he hefted the gun higher.

Taya stiffened, screamed and ducked her head.

Keegan sprang off the steps, jumping to the side.

A blast echoed in the confined space.

Folze fired several more rounds.

Taya prepared to die.

Keegan shielded her body with his, pressing her against the opposite brick wall.

The gunfire stopped, and the overhead door slammed shut, plunging them again into blackness.

"Are you okay?" Keegan asked, his breath warm against her forehead.

She nodded, then realizing he couldn't see her, squeaked, "Yes."

"I'm going to set you down." He placed her on her feet, steadied her, then stepped back.

Submerged in the inkiness, Taya fought her rising panic. Unable to see her hand in front of her face—not that the restraints allowed for it—she focused her other senses.

He moved around, shuffling for something.

The pressure built and before she could control it, Taya cried out, "Keegan!"

She hated the weak childlike screech, but rationale blew away in the crushing darkness. Terror returned, smothering her, compounded by her bound wrists and ankles.

Keegan's strong hand gripped her shoulder, his tone gentle and reassuring. "I'm here."

Two words that soothed her heart and comforted her soul.

A hiccup escaped, adding to her pitifulness.

He turned on the flashlight, and a soft glow filled the room. "Sorry it took me so long. I dropped it when I jumped."

She was the one who should be apologizing. Taya inhaled and exhaled a few more times, calming herself. She sniffled, embarrassed. Humiliated. What must he think of her? "Forgive me. The dark is just—"

"Another thing you're not a fan of, huh?"

A smile tugged at her lips, but she didn't have the strength to follow through. She recalled he'd said the same thing about her attitude toward law enforcement.

She still felt that way—Folze was proof corrupt cops existed. Except she couldn't deny Keegan infiltrated her rock-solid point of view. Unlike anyone she'd ever known.

Nothing like Jeremy.

Nothing like Folze.

Keegan was...different.

"Fears aren't rational. Helps to talk about them, though."

Taya swallowed. He shifted the light and she caught sight of blood on his hand. Dripping from his shoulder. "You're hurt!"

"Just a bullet grazing, thanks to my stealthy moves," he teased, glancing at the wound.

The sound of heavy thuds against the door interrupted him.

"He's barricading us in," Taya guessed.

"Sounds like it," Keegan replied, facing the door. He rushed up the stairs and with a guttural sound, tackled the door. He turned and, using his back, continued to slam against it, producing sickening thuds, but it didn't budge.

Each thrust added to Taya's overwhelming headache.

An engine fired up, then faded into the distance.

"He's gone." Her interpretation of the obvious snapped Keegan from his war with the door.

He gave the barricade one last thud before descending the stairs. "I should've charged through him before he closed the door."

"I don't doubt your abilities, but maybe take a short break from ramming the door."

Sweat streaked his face and hairline. "I just need a minute."

"He'd have killed you."

"Nah. His shooting is less than accurate considering he missed all four times," Keegan grunted with a lopsided grin. "Maybe I should've gone for the kinder, gentler approach."

That brought a smile to her lips. "Somehow, I don't think that would've mattered."

"Yeah, I suppose you're right. Maybe he's the kind of guy who needs a hug and understanding."

A chuckle escaped. "If you remove these zip ties, I'll help you find something to break through the door." Taya appreciated Keegan's good-natured manner. Within a few minutes, he'd calmed her.

"Right. Sorry I got sidetracked." In a single move, Keegan lifted her into his arms.

Taya didn't miss the slight wince, though he carried her to the steps without complaint and gently set her down. She sat while he adjusted the flashlight, aiming it upward, then withdrew a small knife from inside his boot.

"Always prepared?"

"Yep, part of my childhood summer camp training." He slipped the knife under the ankle zip tie and gave a tug, breaking it free. "One down. Now if you'll twist around, I can get to the one on your wrist."

She obeyed and after a quick pass of the blade, the restraints snapped off. "You did it! Thank you."

Blood streaked Keegan's hand.

"Let me get a look at your shoulder," she said.

"It's fine."

"Keegan." She used the tone saved for the rowdiest of her college anthropology students.

He shrugged out of the jacket and rolled up the shirtsleeve. Taya shifted into doctor mode, ignoring his muscular physique, and aimed her attention at his wound. "It's a significant laceration. I'd recommend stitches. For now, do you see anything we can apply to stop the bleeding?" She reached into her coat pocket, grazing a small object. "In our rush to leave Ashfall, I didn't log this," she confessed, holding up the bullet casing.

"Better to keep it in your possession anyway," Keegan affirmed, then looked down, inspecting the injury. "That's just a scrape. It'll be fine." He pulled on his shirt and jacket.

Stubborn man. She pushed the casing into her pocket and zipped it closed, ensuring she wouldn't lose it. "How did you find me? Is Bear alive?"

Keegan launched into a hurried explanation about finding Bear unconscious. "If Wanda hadn't warned me about my blown cover, I would've never arrived in time to give him the Narcan."

"She saved both your lives."

He blew out a breath. "Yes, she did. All right, let's compare notes. Your turn. Start at the beginning. What happened after I left?"

Taya shared her terrifying encounter with Folze. "I have

a confession. I've only shot a gun a couple of times and never at another human being."

He nodded as if he'd already figured that out. "Did you hesitate?"

"No. I guess survival instincts kicked in. I pulled the trigger. Except I forgot to remove the safety."

"I shouldn't have assumed you were comfortable with a weapon."

"You're not to blame. It was my pride. I didn't want to appear incompetent."

Keegan leaned closer. "Taya, you're the furthest thing from incompetent."

She shrugged, straightening her posture. "I could've killed him." Her voice faded, contemplating the reality. Keegan remained silent, and she continued rattling off the entire wretched event. "I awakened in Folze's pickup and heard him talking to Brando. He demanded more money and offered to…" she paused, hating her quivering voice "…'take care of me.' Brando told him Vice would do it."

Keegan's head jerked up. "He said 'Vice'?"

"Yes." She searched his eyes. "Who's that?"

Keegan swallowed. "His real name is Vern Zilner. His rap sheet is an extensive list of everything from petty crime to murder. Vice is Brando's cleanup guy."

"He'll kill Folze?"

"In a heartbeat. Once Brando has you, the SIM card and the remains, Folze will have served his purpose. Removing him is the logical next step."

"He didn't appear upset by the instructions."

"Then he's stupider or more manipulative than I thought. By dividing the evidence, it gives him time to negotiate. Or he's planning to bluff his way out of it and get away. Brando's men already searched the house here, so Folze's got the evidence hidden somewhere else."

Taya relayed the rest of the conversation she'd overheard. "I guess it's a good thing I was unconscious and had tape covering my mouth. If I'd screamed, Brando's men might've found me before you did."

"I don't know what I'd have done if I hadn't found you." His husky tone and penetrating gaze held Taya.

"Thank you for not giving up on me." Her eyes traveled over his face to his jaw.

His Adam's apple bobbed and he leaned closer. His breath was warm on her face.

"The shelves," she blurted.

He jerked back and cleared his throat. "What?"

"We can use them like a battering ram."

"Oh, right. Find a short plank."

She pushed off the stair and dug through the wood, needing distance from him before she did something stupid. And immediately hated the absence from him. "Folze told Brando to meet him at his cabin."

"I found a car registration with an address in Running Water, South Dakota. That's located on the other side of Chief Standing Bear Bridge, roughly 45 minutes away. I'm guessing that's the cabin. Did they discuss a time?"

Taya thought back to the conversation. "No."

"The door is old and rotted. It's splintered but not giving way. Whatever he's got on top of it is holding tight."

"Right." She backed up, unexpectedly kicking something hard. "What on earth? Keegan, can you bring the flashlight closer?"

He moved beside her and searched the rubble at her feet, finally withdrawing a small black fireproof box. "Ah." Then, digging into his pocket, he removed a piece of paper with numbers scrawled on it.

"Found this in the house," he explained. He entered the digits into the safe's keypad and the lock released. Keegan opened the lid, revealing rolls of money. He closed the safe and passed it to her. "We're taking it with us."

Taya found a sturdy plank, and Keegan rushed up the stairs, ramming the wood into the door. After several more thrusts, a crack resounded.

"It's working!" Taya exclaimed.

"No, he's got something on the door." Keegan shifted positions and, holding the shelf in an upright manner, pushed up, forcing it partially open.

"Go through!" he grunted, propping the door open with the wood plank.

Taya climbed out and turned back to him. "Folze placed more wood planks lengthwise over the door and added sandbags to hold them down. Give me a second." She dragged off a sandbag.

Keegan thrust open the door and climbed through, carrying the money box.

They ran through the trees where Bear's old pickup sat, all four tires flattened. Keegan slammed his hand on the hood, startling her. "When I get my hands on Folze—"

"Is there another vehicle?"

"You're brilliant." He ran toward the last Quonset and Taya rushed to catch up. Inside sat Folze's game and parks pickup. "He traded his truck for his sports car."

"What sports car?" she asked, confused.

"Long story."

"How kind of him to leave us a ride," she quipped, climbing into the passenger side.

"And to leave us the keys," Keegan added, gesturing to the ring hanging from the ignition.

He pulled out a cell phone and paper. "Enter the address into the GPS."

She did, passed him the phone, and he studied the screen. "I'll take you to the sheriff's office. I'm not risking your life again."

Taya crossed her arms. "Don't even go there. Face it, you need my help. We're finishing this. Together."

An argument lingered in his stormy eyes, then morphed into a grin. "I had to do the gentlemanly thing and offer you an out."

She rolled her eyes, but a smile played on her lips.

He extended his hand. "Challenge extended."

Taya grasped his hand and gave it a hearty shake. "Challenge accepted."

TEN

Keegan focused on the blurred yellow lines, his thoughts jostling between fury at Folze and amazement at Taya's fortitude. She'd been attacked, shot with a Taser and tranquilizer gun, left in a pitch-dark root cellar and bounced back, more determined than before.

"I don't remember if I thanked you." Taya reached up and fingered her blood-caked hair and bruised face. Both testimony of a struggle she never should've had to fight.

Sarcasm? No. The appreciation was legitimate and undeserved. "You should be furious with me. Are you sure you're okay?"

"Other than the brain-shaking headache, I'm fine. The wound was superficial and stopped bleeding a while ago."

"Taya, I'm so sorry."

"For what? You've done nothing wrong. I'd have escaped if I'd remember the safety and watched where I was going down the stairs. I've learned valuable lessons in all of this."

"Care to share?"

"For one, I never want to experience a Taser again. It was the worst sensation! I was conscious but unable to move."

"That's the idea. The electricity stops the person in their tracks and gives the officers time to apprehend them," Keegan said flatly. Why was he spouting useless information? Anything to silence the guilt trip looping on an endless reel in his mind.

"Two, when this is all over, I'm learning how to shoot a gun."

Keegan grinned. "I love your moxie."

"Change the things you can and all that."

An interesting comment. "What can't you change?"

Taya turned away, muffling her voice. "Fears."

He recalled her reaction in the cellar and probed, "You mean like the dark?"

"Yes."

"It's possible to overcome anything with God."

Taya snorted. "Maybe. Let's just forget about it."

"Nope, either you talk to me, or you're singing. I need background noise. It'll make the time go faster for both of us."

She hesitated, and Keegan wondered if he'd pushed too hard.

"When I was a kid, I got locked in our farmhouse attic for a night, sometime before Christmas."

"How old were you?"

"Ten."

"By accident?" He refrained from looking at her, afraid she'd clam up.

"My parents went out of town for the evening. I was supposed to stay at my friend's house, but I overheard my sisters planning a secret party and hid in the attic. Figured I'd surprise them."

Keegan chuckled. "I'm sure they loved that."

"Definitely not. They're nine and eleven years older than me. I'm the quintessential annoying little sister."

Patrice bounced to the forefront of his mind, and his throat tightened.

"My flashlight battery died, and I rushed to the door. I didn't realize it locked from the outside. The music was so loud, no one heard me. I cried myself to sleep and spent the whole night trapped in the dark. My parents came home early the next morning and found me."

"Did your sisters get in trouble?"

"Yep, grounded for months."

Keegan's heart tugged for young Taya. "Poor kid. You must've been terrified."

She was so quiet, he looked over to see if she was okay. He gave her shoulder a one-handed squeeze.

"Thank you," she said.

"For what?"

"For not making fun of me."

He hadn't expected that.

"Jeremy never understood. He laughed and told me to get over it," she explained.

Ol' Jeremy gained points by the second. "I'd never do that to you." His hand was still on her shoulder.

"I don't doubt you." She gave him a small smile. "I have another confession, though."

"Okay."

"When Folze kidnapped me, I was angry with you. With Bear. I wondered if they were in cahoots. My suspicions went all over the place."

Lord, give me wisdom. "In all fairness, we view things through our lens of experience. Considering the hurt you've endured, it's understandable. Truthfully, it wasn't fair of us to ask you to trust two strangers."

"Agreed, and normally, I wouldn't have. Although, none of this has been normal. Evaluating facts makes me competent in my vocation. Still, there's no benefit in equivocating the truth. I've unfairly placed blame on all law enforcement officers for Jeremy's misdeeds."

A vulnerable confession layered in her shield of intelligence. "Fair enough. Brutal truth? *Jaded* might better describe your outlook." Keegan softened the admonishment with his best encouraging smile.

She shook her head. "As a scientist, I cannot condone that attitude."

"I'd say this falls into the 'change the things you can' category. You said you like fresh starts. This is a great way to begin the new year. Choose to think the best first."

"Your comment coincides with something I recently read in my Bible study about thinking on good, worthy things."

"Philippians 4:8?"

She smiled. "Very impressive."

"Years of sword drills in Sunday school."

Taya recognized the phrase referring to a Bible game she'd played as a child. "Because of the evil you deal with, isn't it hard to be a man of faith? You can't just turn the other cheek. How do you prevent becoming jaded with the less than desirable people you encounter?"

"Looking for advice?"

She grinned. "Perhaps."

"Law enforcement officers are peacekeepers. We bear the burden of tough split-second, life-altering calls so it's a delicate balance. We choose to serve the public by willingly laying down our lives to protect the innocent and ensure order. Admittedly, it's not always clear who is for or against us. I can't assume everyone's a criminal or take every person at face value. I suppose it's a skill developed over time."

"You're a wise man, Keegan Stryker."

He chuckled. "I wouldn't go that far." The timing couldn't be worse, but he liked the woman behind the intellectual mask more every minute they were together. When the case concluded—and it would tonight, it had to—he'd never see her again. They'd go their separate ways.

He wasn't ready for that to happen. "Taya, I've never met anyone like you."

"I echo those sentiments."

Hope bounded. Outstanding. She felt the same connection. Ignoring the past-relationship warning he'd clung to, he said, "Do share."

"I spend the majority of my time in a laboratory setting or in front of a classroom filled with eager college students. I can say without reservation this has been the most adventurous time of my life. I'm not accustomed to working perilous weapons trafficking cases with an undercover ATF agent."

Keegan chuckled, gaining courage. "You're the first anthropologist I've had the pleasure of meeting."

"We've got one bright spot in this nightmare. Our heroic acts will be the stuff of legends in both our fields," she teased.

"I'm hoping our ties don't end with the case." He plunged forward before his bravery depleted. "I'd love to get to know you better. Once we're safe and not in the middle of life-threatening danger," he added.

Dead silence.

The comment sucked all the prior openness from the atmosphere and replaced it with an awkward lull.

A tingle swept up the back of his neck and across his face, burning his cheeks. Afraid to speak, he glimpsed at Taya. She stared straight ahead.

Fantastic. Say something. Anything. "Sorry. That came out totally wrong."

Taya remained quiet for several horrendous seconds before clearing her throat and addressing him. The bogus smile she wore faded into an expression lingering somewhere between pity and surprise.

In a word. Rejection. Desperate to save the minuscule pieces of his dignity, he said, "Forget I said anything."

"Keegan." Her placating tone shrank him in the seat. "Of course we'll keep in touch after you return to *Missouri*."

Did he imagine the hiss in her voice on the last word?

"I've enjoyed our talks and I'd like to be friends."

Ouch. That was worse than having her shoot him down in flames. Why had he said anything?

Eyes glued to the road, Keegan replayed the conversation, honing in on her emphasis of him returning to Missouri. He recalled her abrupt dismissal at the school as soon as he mentioned the promotion opportunity. She'd clarified how she'd never conform to the wishes of any man after Jeremy's betrayal. *The changes it would've required are more than I care to make at this stage in my life. Besides I've already given up too much. I've no desire to do that, especially not for a man.* Bitter words to cover up her real dream of working for the FBI?

"I hope I've not offended you," she went on. "You're a wonderful person and I appreciate all you've done."

Keegan tried to laugh it off, but he emitted a strange mixture of grunt and cough. "No. Not at all."

For a mile, neither spoke.

"How much farther to the cabin?" Taya asked, erecting that invisible wall between them.

"About a half hour." Thirty long what-are-we-supposed-to-talk-about-now minutes.

"I've never heard of the town Running Water."

Grateful for the change of topics, Keegan explained finding the pictures and homing in on the sign over Chief Standing Bear Bridge.

"I remember studying the trial of Standing Bear in my college Native American history course. He fought one of the most infamous legal battles in 1879."

He'd forced the poor woman into rambling historical facts for the sake of conversation?

Taya continued, "Standing Bear carried the bones of his

sixteen-year-old son for two winter months, trekking the Great Plains. Then he was arrested, all for wanting to bury his son on their native land." She sighed. "Kind of ironic, isn't it? We're battling to recover Patrice's remains in the same location in the same wintry season."

"Did he win the battle?"

"Yes, in May that same year."

"If we've got any hope of victory in this war, we need to work on our plan of action, starting with what arsenal we have. If Folze's got company, surprise and darkness are our only advantages. Would you mind hopping in the back and checking for any other weapons? Maybe he left us his tranquilizer or Taser guns, too."

Taya grunted, climbing into the back seat. "Unless he added a bunch after tossing me in the root cellar, I doubt there's anything here." A few moments of rustling, then she said, "Nope. Nothing but a locked toolbox and zip ties."

Not good odds. "Okay, that leaves us with two guns and one extra magazine."

She returned to her seat. "What about your team?"

Keegan gripped the steering wheel, debating the same question. "Not yet."

"But we need backup, don't you agree?"

In a word. Yes.

"What's your hesitation?" Taya probed.

"If there's a leak in the ATF, they'd send word, giving Folze opportunity to escape, or worse, we drive into an ambush."

"You're absolutely right. I hadn't considered those outcomes."

Keegan grinned. "I'm sorry." He lifted Bear's cell phone and held it out to her. "Could you repeat that louder into the voice recorder?"

She laughed. "Nope. That was a single declaration."

He chuckled. "Can't blame a guy for trying."

They rode in silence, Keegan working through scenarios that amped his anxiety. Once more, he contemplated calling Hawk for backup. Then quickly talked himself out of it. The fear of losing Taya sickened his stomach. He'd prefer she was somewhere far away. But there was no one else to call, and he wouldn't leave her again.

"I'm afraid to ask what's kept you quiet for so long," Taya said, interrupting his thoughts.

"I'm working through our tactical ops."

"And what're we doing?"

"Best-case scenario, Folze's alone and we overpower him."

"Worse case?"

"Brando's men outnumber us. I'll do recon before we proceed, but Taya, you have to be honest with me. If you're not comfortable covering me, say so. Hesitation is worse than absence."

"I understand. I'm confident I can do what has to be done," she replied.

He prayed she was right. "I also have a contingency plan."

"Oh, yes, no good takedown is complete without one of those."

Keegan sensed the nervousness behind her teasing tone. "Should something go wrong and we lose control of the situation, we need a few code phrases. For example, if you're held hostage—"

She gasped. "What? Why would that happen?"

"We're processing situations."

"Fine."

"If I tell you to 'drop dead' or use those two words in conjunction, go wheels up."

"I don't understand that connotation."

"Sorry, it's cop slang. It means drop to the ground. If

someone's holding you, relax. They won't expect to hold dead weight."

"Oh. Why not just say that?"

"I did." He grinned. "It'll take the person off guard. They're expecting you to resist and fight back. When you fall, it'll get you out of the way and provide an opening to make the necessary shot."

"I'm not implying you're not a qualified marksman, but what if you accidentally shoot me?"

"Trust me." Tall order considering their short history…

"This isn't instilling confidence in me."

"We're preparing for the worst, hoping for the best."

"I suppose." Taya crossed her arms. "And what's the best?"

"Folze hands over the evidence, Brando quietly surrenders—"

"—and we all live happily ever after," Taya said with a guffaw.

There was a greater chance a meteor would hit Folze's cabin before they got there, but he didn't share that.

Relieved by Keegan's take-charge attitude and the opportunity to skip past the awkward moment they'd shared, Taya pondered her quick reaction to his comment. He'd not finished speaking before she jumped in and eliminated the discussion. Had she prematurely predicted where he was going?

Heat warmed her neck, and she worried she'd misread his intentions. *Taya, I've never met anyone like you. Once this over, and we're not in the middle of life-threatening danger, I'd love to get to know you better.*

She glanced at him then averted her eyes. No, his comment was a test, an effort to gauge her attraction. She'd handled the situation with the appropriate nonemotional response. He'd not pressed the issue, further confirmation she'd accurately interpreted his objective.

So, why did she feel so lousy? The answer was so plain before her she couldn't argue if she wanted to—her feelings for Keegan were developing, too. As much as she longed for this unbelievable disaster of a mess to end, it meant never seeing him again. Sure, they'd have interactions for judicial proceedings but that wasn't the same.

Though psychology wasn't a field that intrigued her, she'd once read about law enforcement and military men with the propensity to attract needy women. Her pathetic and childish fears had morphed her into a persona befitting that description. Taya disciplined herself to exude confidence, yet in those weak moments, she'd eliminated that persona. A new loathing cloaked her.

Truth be told, she was tired of wearing a mask to hide her insecurities. Keegan made her feel safe and intelligent. He hadn't ridiculed her or shown disdain for her childhood confessions. His acceptance propelled her to share more, but she squelched the urge. Granting him further access into her vulnerabilities was a recipe for disaster.

She'd not reveal the actual reason for refusing his offer of more than friendship. Her interruption had been a kindness. A great man like Keegan would tire of an unattractive nerd who buried herself in academics to disguise her insecurities. Her rejection saved them both the trouble of a bad breakup.

Liar. She cringed at the excuses and the accuracy of her conscience's assessment. She was too much of a mess for anyone to take on. Even Keegan.

Yet, he intrigued her. His valor came packaged as the most exquisite gentleman—a fierce and uncommon combination. Keegan was like discovering gifts she'd never known she wanted. Realizing he was everything she needed.

The possibility thrilled and terrified her. She'd not survive another heartbreak. And if it was possible, she was falling harder for him than she had for Jeremy. Whatever Keegan did to her insides ensured that she'd face-plant without recovering if their relationship didn't work out.

There was no future outside of friendship for them.

A truth woven in a lie, but it had to be said.

So why did she desperately want to take back the words?

Taya fisted her hands, containing her internal battle. Regardless, he'd made clear his intentions to return to Missouri for the sake of his promotion. He deserved great things. She'd be a weight dragging him down. And once he figured that out, he'd leave her.

No, she'd not give up her life for any man. Taya renewed her internal vow and tucked her heart inside its lonely protective cover.

Except what kind of life was she hanging on to? She existed in a depressing and isolated cocoon. A reality she'd not admit to anyone, especially her judgmental siblings who viewed her as the spinster sister.

Enough. The contemplations were useless and unproductive.

The deafening silence prodded Taya to initiate communication again, but topics eluded her.

The truck's rumbling engine filled the cab. Darkness veiled the waters, and a brown sign on the side announced Chief Standing Bear Memorial Bridge, Missouri National Recreational River. No traffic accompanied them as they crossed from Nebraska into South Dakota via the expansive two-lane bridge.

A new wave of embarrassment smacked into her. Had she really rambled on about Nebraska history? Taya gave herself a mental slap to the forehead and slumped down in the seat. If there was a way to make a total and complete idiot of herself, she'd scored bonus points with that move.

Keegan's phone rang, startling her.

Taya sent a prayer of gratitude for the timely interruption.

"Bear, are you on the mend?" Keegan listened, his expression unwavering.

Taya leaned closer to eavesdrop but he moved the cell in his left hand. She harrumphed and crossed her arms.

A long pause.

"Now what?" she inquired.

Keegan's forehead creased, and he worked his jaw. "Are you sure? Maybe—" He sighed. "No, you're right. Okay, thanks."

Curiosity swimming in her stomach, Taya looked for an approaching vehicle or other deadly hazard. What had happened?

She gaped at Keegan's next revelation. "Folze's got a cabin on the other side of the Missouri River," he told Bear. "Headed there."

Why had he revealed that? Would Bear provide backup for them?

"Can't. Not yet. I'll be in touch. Soon." Keegan disconnected and slipped the phone into his jacket pocket.

Can't what?

Eyes fixated on the road, he remained silent.

Taya's anxiety ratcheted at his lack of communication. At the threat of bursting, she asked, "Keegan, what's wrong?"

It took several extensive seconds before he responded, "Wanda's missing."

Taya gasped. "Brando discovered she warned you. Would he—" She couldn't speak the dreaded question when she already knew the answer. Brando wouldn't waste time holding Wanda prisoner. He'd eliminate her.

Patrice's ring came to mind, with the symbolic parental butterflies. Taya's chest tightened, and her throat thickened with emotion. When would the deaths stop? She squeezed her eyes shut. *Please, Lord, end this nightmare.* "What will happen to her daughter, Molly?"

He didn't answer. The child would be left in the system. Orphaned.

Keegan's dark countenance held foreboding. He'd confessed how he blamed himself for Patrice's death. Was he adding Wanda to that internal flogging? She'd accepted the risks of acting as a confidential informant.

Love for her child motivated her past the danger. She'd jeopardized everything by warning Keegan away from the meeting with Brando. And she'd died as a result.

Taya's heart ached and she longed to speak comfort. Nothing she offered would help. *Lord, You alone will bring good out of Patrice and Wanda's sacrifices.*

Between the devastating news about Wanda and Taya's immediate rejection of Keegan's advances, the atmosphere nearly smothered her.

Out of the darkness, LED headlights beamed at them from the oncoming lane. The newer pickup blasted by, its stereo booming with enough bass to shake the windows.

Taya watched it speed toward the Nebraska border, disappearing into the inky distance.

Keegan said nothing as he turned off the highway onto a winding road that paralleled the river. The elevation inclined as the road wove through forested country, taking them deeper into secluded land. The terrain grew rougher and evergreens heavy with snow bordered them on either side. Taya gripped the door handle, tension infusing her muscles.

"How will we know where Folze's—" Her words fell flat as Keegan rounded the corner and approached a clearing.

Towering flames stretched into the night sky. The rectangular cabin, roughly twenty by thirty feet, was ablaze.

Colorful Christmas lights hung from the eaves encircling the wraparound porch. A bright red sports car sat nearby.

"So much for recon," Keegan said, parking the truck.

"Do you think Folze's still inside?" Taya leaned forward, fingers digging into the dashboard.

"There's a good possibility."

She scanned the property. "Are we in danger?"

"I'm guessing whoever set the fire didn't intend to hang around." Keegan shifted his gaze to her, reaching into his jacket and passing her a pistol. "The safety is off so be careful. Trade places with me and stay in the truck. I'll go look for Folze."

She started to argue, but he was out and running toward the cabin before she'd unsnapped her seat belt.

Taya exited the pickup and tugged open the back door, searching for something to help him. Her gaze landed on a silver package, and she pulled it from the seat pocket. Large black letters read Fire Retardant Blanket. Perfect.

Blanket and gun in hand, she rushed to assist Keegan.

Intense heat and smoke consumed the perimeter and Taya struggled to breathe. Pressing on, she ran to the back of the house where Keegan stood beside a broken window.

He turned at her approach, frustration etched on his handsome face. "I told you—"

"You'll need this," she interrupted, shoving the blanket at him.

Keegan grasped the package and ripped it open, removing the blanket. "Great thinking. Cover me." He nodded toward her weapon. "Don't be afraid to shoot anyone who shows up."

"Got it," she called over the roaring flames.

Cloaked under the fire-resistant material, he climbed through the window.

Taya watched until he disappeared into the smoke. Eyes and nose burning, she ducked her face inside her coat. She held the gun with the delicacy of a live bomb, prepared to pull the trigger.

Dirty snow drifts peaked on the edges of the clearing, reminding her of Grammy McGill's lemon meringue pie. A shelterbelt of evergreens protected the home from the north winds. All clearly visible courtesy of the orange-and-yellow flames clawing their way from the entrance of the cabin.

Seconds dragged out like hours.

Was Keegan okay? She shifted impatiently from one foot to another, contemplating whether to follow him. What if she got turned around and trapped inside? She'd do more damage by making him rescue her, too. He'd told her to cover him. She was his backup. The rationalizations combined with the emitting heat and smoke kept her wary and frozen in place.

If Folze was dead, how would they find Patrice's remains? And what about the SIM card? Without the wretched man, they'd be back to square one without any leads.

She turned toward the burning cabin, beseeching Keegan and Folze to emerge.

Please, Lord, help him.

ELEVEN

Keegan rushed through the burning house hunched under the blanket. Smoke stung his eyes, blurring his vision. He spotted Folze hog-tied on the floor in the center of the living room and sprinted to his side.

"Help me," the officer rasped, amazement and confusion mingling in the one eye not swollen shut.

Keegan knelt and, using the knife from his boot, swiped through the bindings. He threw the blanket over Folze and hefted him up. Together, they hurried to the bedroom.

The loft beams crumbled, collapsing where they'd stood only seconds before.

"Taya!" He shoved Folze toward the window.

The injured man attempted to climb out. His large form consumed most of the opening. After several failed attempts, Folze squeezed through and Keegan followed close behind. The trio rushed from the burning house to the safety of the ground beside the pickup.

Folze stumbled and fell to his knees, hacking from the smoke, but Keegan refused to give him an inch. Gun trained, he waited for Folze to recover and glanced at Taya, nose tucked into her sleeve, coughing.

"Are you okay?"

She nodded, waving him off.

Folze sat back on his heels. His dirty, bruised and bleeding face testified to a severe beating. "You escaped," he rasped.

"No thanks to you."

Folze raised his hands. "Please don't kill me."

"Yeah, I saved you from a raging fire to shoot you myself," Keegan snapped.

"Why did you help me?" His gaze bounced between Taya and Keegan. "I didn't want to do it. Brando forced me—"

"Liar!" Taya stepped forward, hovering over the blubbering officer. "I heard everything. Where are Patrice's remains and the SIM card?"

"I—I don't know what you mean," Folze stuttered.

Keegan's hand shook with adrenaline, but he retained control. "Where are they?"

"Vice torched my beautiful cabin."

"I'm fresh out of sympathy," Keegan said.

Folze exhaled. "Brando owes me money. He'll pay, and I'll split it with you."

Unbelievable. Folze's greed overrode his common sense. "You really don't get it, do you? When they find out you're still alive, Vice will return to finish you."

Folze shook his head, jowls quivering. "No. Don't let them hurt me. I'll tell you everything."

"I'm listening," Keegan pressed.

"I buried her at Ashfall. Figured it was the safest place to hide her. No one would think to look in the same place. Brando offered more money if I took you out, Agent Stryker."

"We'd have seen a freshly dug grave when we searched there," Taya contended.

Folze shook his head. "I did it after I took you to the cellar."

"That's why you left and returned," Keegan concluded.

"Had to get my car," Folze replied, shame or regret—Keegan wasn't certain which—covered his face.

"Where?" Taya intervened.

Folze put both hands on his thighs, shoulders rounded. "Near the Rhino Barn on the far south side." He paused. "Thing is…"

"What?" Keegan barked. "Speak!"

"There's a weapons delivery scheduled tonight. We'd have to hurry, but we could make it. Get out of there before Brando arrives."

Taya studied the man. "He's probably lying."

Folze shrugged. "It's risky. Better wait until tomorrow, when you won't have any chance of running into Brando's men."

"Where's the SIM card?" Taya asked.

"If I tell you, will you let me go?"

"You're an idiot," Keegan huffed.

Folze sighed, sending him into another coughing attack. He heaved a breath. "My boot."

"Lie flat on your stomach, hands behind your back."

The man maneuvered himself prone, then lifted his head. "Agent Stryker, please don't turn me into the cops yet. Let me help you. I owe you both that much."

"Check his boot. One wrong twitch and I'll shoot him," Keegan said.

Taya hesitated, turned and walked to the truck. She returned wearing plastic gloves and carrying zip ties. "Security measure."

Keegan grinned.

"Which foot?" she asked.

"Right," Folze answered, lifting the appendage.

She zip tied Folze's wrists behind his back, then tugged off his boot and flipped it upside down. A small SIM card fell out. She held it up and gave Keegan a nod.

Folze's double-talk might be a setup to walk them

into an ambush. But why do that when Vice had almost killed him? If there was a delivery, Keegan could take down Brando, ending this whole nightmare. The positive outcome—however uncertain as it was—outweighed the risks. He must get to Ashfall.

"Keegan?" Taya pressed.

"I'm hesitant to trust a liar, but we're running out of time. I have to recover Patrice, and we'll hand Folze over to the authorities."

Sirens wailed in the distance.

"We have to get out of here before the fire department shows up and starts asking a lot of questions." Keegan helped Folze to his feet while Taya opened the rear passenger door.

Folze scooted in and Taya entered the front seat, shifting to keep her gun trained on him.

"If he so much as wrinkles his nose, shoot him."

"Not a problem." The disgust written in her expression said she meant it.

Jumping into the driver's seat, Keegan sped off the property. "What time is the delivery?"

"Ten thirty at Ashfall."

"You've used Ashfall for trafficking weapons?" Taya asked, her tone incredulous.

Folze grunted. "It's perfect because it's closed all winter. And since I'm the one assigned the region, they have guaranteed security."

"You should be ashamed of yourself," Taya retorted.

"You don't understand. For the first time ever, I had money. I could buy big things," Folze whined.

"No matter what it cost anyone?"

Keegan glanced in the mirror, meeting Folze's eyes.

"Why did you save my life?"

"Folze, you're a cockroach and an embarrassment to the badge, but I'll let a judge determine your fate."

"That's better than Vice killing me," Folze grumbled.

The reminder that Brando's army outnumbered them slapped Keegan with a reality check. No more Lone Ranger rescues—he needed backup.

He reached for Bear's phone and dialed.

"Stryker! Are you all right?" Hawk blurted after two rings.

"I have Folze in custody. Brando's men did a number on him."

"Where are you?"

"Headed to Ashfall."

"Why?"

Keegan relayed the details Folze had shared about re-burying Patrice there and the traffickers' next delivery. "I need backup ASAP. It's the perfect chance to take down Brando. This is it."

"Outstanding! Let me get everything into place."

"One more thing. Vice hog-tied Folze before torching his cabin."

"Like Skull," Hawk said, piecing together the evidence. "I'll be in touch." He disconnected.

Keegan concentrated on playing out the scenario in his mind.

They crossed Chief Standing Bear Bridge, and the phone rang. Hawk.

"That was fast."

"We have a problem."

"Why doesn't that surprise me?"

"Hazardous material spill from an overturned semi closed the main highway. We're taking a detour, but doubtful we'll get there before the delivery. Stand down. We'll get him next time."

"Negative." No way was Keegan letting Brando get away.

"I'll testify," Folze hollered from the back seat.

"Shut up," Keegan barked.

"Can Folze identify Brando?" Hawk asked.

Keegan relayed the question.

Folze hesitated, adding to Keegan's suspicions. "Sort of."

"No, he can't. See, boss? This has to happen today. I'll get there ahead of them. Surprise attack."

"And what if there's twenty men? You're going to take on an army alone?"

"Taya and I—"

"You are not using a civilian in this. Absolutely not! Stand down, Stryker, that's an order. Folze's testimony will help. We will find Brando."

"I have to at least get a picture, so I can prove who he is." *And if there's any chance of taking him down, I'm doing it.* But Keegan didn't offer that piece of information. "Get there as fast as you can."

"Nebraska State Patrol has a helicopter. I'll see if they'll work with us."

Cooperative agency help was a benefit, unless you weren't sure who to trust. "Maybe we shouldn't bring anyone else into this."

"Stryker—"

Keegan lowered his voice and turned on the radio so Folze wouldn't be able to hear him. "Brando knows my identity. Wanda warned me and now she's missing."

"CIs are notoriously unreliable liars."

"Wanda has always been dependable, and she saved my life. Bear's, too."

"I don't like what you're implying. We have plenty of public distrust and accusations against us. We don't need our own pointing a suspicious finger, too."

"There's a mole."

Hawk sighed. "Stryker, if I had any concern about the integrity of our team, I'd arrest them myself."

Keegan considered the group. Not all friends, but no one stood out as a traitor. "I don't think it's on our side."

"DEA?"

"Possibly," Keegan agreed.

"I can't go charging into the DEA's office accusing them without proof," Hawk contended.

"We don't have much choice."

"I'll keep the need to know limited and take the heat for not sharing later. I'll be in touch." Hawk disconnected.

"Well? Now what?" Taya asked, turning down the radio.

"I drop you two off at the state patrol's office. My team will meet you and take Folze into custody."

"And you're facing Brando alone? No way. I'm in this."

Keegan studied her. "Taya, I can't risk your life. You've danced with death too many times for my comfort. Please. I need you to watch Folze."

"I won't go anywhere," Folze whined.

"Save it," Keegan answered.

Folze leaned back in the seat with a huff.

"Keegan, we have to work together. You need me."

More than she could ever imagine. "I can't argue with that logic."

"Patrice deserves justice, and I won't sleep until that happens. I have a job to do, and I intend to finish it."

His heart tugged at her confession. "Yes, ma'am," he said with a grin. "Folze, here's your chance to prove you're not the scum I think you are."

"If I do what you want, will you cut me a deal?"

The man was incorrigible.

Within twenty minutes, Keegan was traversing a minimum maintenance lane leading to the backside of Ashfall, grateful for the four-wheel-drive truck's agility. He parked in the valley beneath a cluster of trees.

"We'll walk the rest of the way. Folze, be a good boy

and stay put in the pickup's tailgate shell topper. Where's the key for it?"

"In the console," he replied.

The topper covered the bed of the game and park's one-ton truck, and the hatch door locked from the outside. The area was large enough to hold tools and small amounts of equipment. Not ideal, but it'd have to do for now. Keegan retrieved a ring with several keys and climbed out, then assisted Folze out of the back seat.

"Taya, please grab as many zip ties as you can stuff into your coat pockets."

"Got it."

The trio made their way to the rear of the vehicle. Keegan pulled down the tailgate and climbed into the bed. He unlocked the topper door and tugged it open. The interior was sparse except for a toolbox.

"Where will they conduct their business?" Taya asked.

"Outside the Rhino Barn. They'll meet there and make the exchange."

"How many?"

"Two trucks, at least four of Brando's men and four others. They'll be heavily armed. I can help you." Folze was nothing if not persistent.

"No, thanks." Keegan climbed in and, using a smaller key on the ring, unlocked the attached toolbox. He withdrew a small shovel and flashlight, then relocked the toolbox. Exiting the topper, he passed the items to Taya, gave Folze's restraints one last check and ordered him inside. With a second set of zip ties, Keegan secured Folze's hands to a hook in the back.

"This isn't unnecessary, I won't go anywhere," Folze assured.

"Call it a flaw in my personality that I don't trust you."

"I shared the information you asked for. That deserves a reward."

Keegan snorted. "How about a twenty-to-life vacation?"
Folze frowned.

"Just remember, if you try to run away, I'll make it my
personal mission to hunt you down," Keegan warned.

"I got it, I got it." Folze sighed, sitting against the back
wall of the pickup bed.

Keegan exited the topper and locked the door. "Ready?"
Taya hoisted the shovel. "Let's do this."

A half-moon cast soft light, and the atmosphere was
still. Calm and unsettling. Sparse snowflakes fluttered,
peppering their hair. Keegan glanced over his shoulder,
ensuring Folze's work truck remained hidden from view.

Five hundred seventeenth Avenue paralleled the entrance
to the park where the long, winding path ran north, then
curved west, gradually inclining for three-quarters of a
mile into a parking lot, dead-ending at a toolshed. A hand-
ful of outbuildings comprised the facility.

On the east side, a brick single-level structure named
the Guest Center faced the road. A round walkway led to
a smaller building dedicated to rock and tree fossils indig-
enous to the area, and two shelters, one enclosed, the other,
a lean-to used for children's activities.

Keegan and Taya emerged behind the toolshed on the
west side opposite the maintenance building. To the south,
the Rhino Barn—rectangular, comprised of metal and the
largest edifice—faced the road at a northwest angle. A
walking path continued from the corner to a small lean-to
at the outermost edge of the property.

Taya's Winnebago, parked five hundred feet from the
Rhino Barn, provided an additional barrier.

"Do you think Folze will stay put?" she asked, speaking aloud Keegan's doubt.

"Even if he doesn't, he won't get away. He's wanted by
too many people."

"True." Taya faced him, hand on his arm. "Keegan, no

matter what happens tonight, I want you to know you're the most honorable man I've ever met. If this falls apart, I'm grateful for the time we shared." She smiled at him.

The words rattled his confidence. If anything went wrong… Before he overthought his actions, he reached out and drew her close. She melted against him and their lips connected in a moment of appreciation and understanding.

In desperation.

She didn't pull away from his kiss, to his amazement and relief.

They parted, breathless and silent.

Taya took the lead, and he followed. They walked behind her Winnebago, then across the property to the Rhino Barn and along the path to the south side. Hidden from view, they surveyed the ground where Folze claimed he'd buried the remains.

Taya's pace quickened, and she pointed to a section devoid of snow cover. "There, see the disturbed surface?"

Keegan used the small shovel and dug, exposing a banker's box in a shallow grave. He sucked in a breath and paused. The unassuming bland cardboard container concealed the precious cargo inside.

Taya stepped aside, as if she understood the immensity of the moment.

He knelt and gently lifted the box, surprised by the lightness. He held it against his chest and faced Taya, unable to speak. She gave him a nod, conveying her compassion.

Headlights beamed and the hum of an engine destroyed the solace.

He ducked and pulled Taya beside him. "I knew that was too easy. Folze set us up."

"Or they're early," she inserted.

"Doubtful." He scanned the area, homing in on a smaller shelter. The lean-to was less than two hundred yards away. Four feet wide with three walls and an open section opposite the road. If Taya got to it, she'd have the cover to escape into the valley while he dealt with the men.

Cradling the box, Keegan was determined to finish this without backup. He'd convince Taya to go ahead of him and secure the remains.

Keegan passed the container to her and called Hawk.

It rang once, then went silent. The call dropped. No reception.

"I just love rural Nebraska," he grumbled, silencing the device and typed a text message instead. They're here. Need backup now!

When the service reconnected, he prayed it'd send.

Was this the best course? If nothing else, he had to identify Brando. That was all that mattered.

A door slammed, and lights shone from a vehicle hidden from their point of view.

"Stay here." Keegan stayed low and ran along the backside of the building, then peeked around the corner. True to Folze's word, two men stepped out of the black utility van. Keegan recognized the passenger. Vice. The rear doors opened and two others climbed out.

Like circus clowns filing out of a car—in a deadly criminal show—they mingled, talking and laughing, at ease waiting for the exchange.

Keegan returned to Taya. "We need to delay them from leaving and pray Hawk arrives in time."

"What's the plan?"

"They're waiting on the other traffickers." He had to get her out of danger. "Take the remains to the truck. Stay low."

She shook her head. "I'm not leaving without you."

"Secure the remains and check on Folze. Then return. I'll wait for you there." He pointed to the small shelter diagonal from them. "Hopefully by then, backup will arrive."

"I don't know."

"If they get these bones, we've lost the battle."

Taya seemed to consider that and took the box.

"You still have the gun, right?"

She nodded.

"I'll keep watch. Hurry back." He motioned for her to go, then turned away before he changed his mind and begged her to stay.

Taya's lips burned from Keegan's impromptu kiss. The timing was crazy, inappropriate and perfect.

Fingers clutching the precious banker's box, she scurried to the shelter and ducked behind the protective walls, peering out.

Keegan exited the Rhino Barn and crept around the side toward the parking lot.

He'd tricked her, intending to attack Brando's men alone. He'd be killed! No way was she leaving. He needed her help. Even if he was too stubborn to know it.

First, to safely hide the remains. She spotted a stack of cement blocks covered by a tarp wedged in the corner. Upon closer inspection, she found a space big enough for the box along with a small container of odds and ends— including a roll of duct tape, which she stuffed into her pocket. Concealing everything under the tarp, she exited the shelter and trailed Keegan.

Taya halted, the realization as apparent as the handsome man in front of her. She'd follow Keegan Stryker anywhere.

Heart drumming, she increased her pace.

He jerked to face her, wearing a less-than-pleased expression. *Too bad.* He gave her a quizzical glance, as if to say *where's the box?* She pointed to the shelter.

He frowned and turned to watch the intruders.

Taya inched closer to get a better view. The utility van was parked perpendicular to her Winnebago, parallel to where she and Keegan hid. Blacked-out windows concealed the passengers, and the driver stood in front of the vehicle, his back to them.

Keegan motioned for her to stay put and crept toward the unsuspecting criminal. In a stealthy move, he delivered an incapacitating strike. Binding the criminal's wrists and ankles with zip ties, he dragged him around the corner.

Taya ripped off a piece of the duct tape and secured it over the man's mouth, earning an approving grin from Keegan. He removed the man's weapon, tucking it into his jacket pocket and mouthed, *Stay here*, before sliding under the van.

The rear doors swung open, and Taya sucked in a gasp. She scanned the area where Keegan had disappeared, unable to see him in the dark.

Men's voices carried, and she pressed closer to the wall. How long before they discovered their comrade was missing?

She covered her mouth, holding her breath.

A shorter individual wearing a hunter-orange parka walked toward the passenger door. "Vice, gimme a smoke."

Keegan's hand emerged from beneath the van and swept the man's feet. He landed facedown, air whooshing from his lungs. Two swift moves, and he was out.

Keegan was absolutely amazing.

Just as he'd done the first time, he dragged the man to Taya, and they repeated securing him. She removed his gun and passed it to Keegan.

"Dude, c'mon, they're here." The other man beckoned from the opposite side of the vehicle.

"Coming," Keegan responded.

Headlights danced on the road, approaching quickly. Two additional vehicles. An expensive import car and a box truck. Not what Folze had predicted.

Outnumbered, the plan's risk overrode her sense of adventure. Taya waved her hands to get Keegan's attention without attracting the others. He scooted out, glanced her way, then walked to the front and punctured the tires.

He motioned for her to join him, and they ducked beside the van.

"Cover me while they're occupied with the transfer," he whispered.

Taya retrieved her weapon from inside her coat. Hands shaking, she nodded agreement.

Headlights beamed, illuminating her Winnebago. The car pulled up, and the driver jumped out. Tall, lanky and dressed in all black, he turned, his back to them beside his opened door.

"Stay here, keep your eyes on them," Keegan whispered and rushed toward the rear of the van.

Taya returned her gaze to the car as a woman stepped out of the passenger side and paused, hand on the door. Her brown hair was tousled in big waves, framing her narrow face. She stood nearly as tall as the driver and wore a leather coat. Turning, she locked eyes on Taya.

Neither moved.

One daring.

The other warning.

Taya lifted the gun higher, hands still shaking. Could she shoot this woman?

A slam of a door.

"Everyone stop right there!" The familiar voice jerked Taya's attention away from the woman. Folze emerged from the Winnebago. He'd gotten loose! And he held a rifle.

"Brando, come to me, now!" he ordered.

The car's driver glanced at the passenger, then obeyed. Taya gaped. Why would Brando obey Folze? Her mind raced, struggling to piece together the men's behavior.

When he got within reach, Folze snagged him around the throat. Gun swerving at the others, he tugged the driver backward. "Brando, you promised me money."

Had Folze lost his mind?

A blast echoed, acting like a pause button. Everything stopped.

Then, in an instant, gunfire consumed the night.

Keegan yanked Taya behind the Rhino Barn, watching as the men advanced on her Winnebago. Folze returned fire, hitting three of the shooters.

The driver grabbed Folze's arm and spun out of his hold. Several consecutive blasts and Folze crumbled to the ground.

Bright blue-and-red strobes pierced the sky, and the whipping sounds of a helicopter descended in the field beside them.

"Are you okay?" Keegan asked.

Taya nodded.

He ran out from their cover and tackled Brando.

Armed officers emerged from the helicopter. More canvassed the area, appearing from every direction, and surrounded the remaining traffickers.

Taya scanned the scene. Where had the woman gone? Jogging to the south side of the Rhino Barn, Taya spotted her nearing the valley.

I don't think so.

Taya bolted, arms pumping, gun in hand. Her side cramped and her legs grew heavy, but she maintained target lock. Closing the distance, Taya lunged, tackling the woman.

They slammed to the frozen ground, skidding and rolling on the decline. The impact thrust the gun from Taya's hand. She'd landed on the woman's back, holding her down, and refused to let go.

In an instant, their positions switched.

Taya lay faceup, the woman over her. A strike to her face sent stars dancing before Taya's eyes.

Survival instincts took over and Taya thrust her knee

into the woman's stomach, then kicked free from her hold and scurried to her feet.

Not fast enough. The woman delivered a roundhouse kick to the side of Taya's head, sending her stumbling back.

Undeterred, Taya rushed forward and swung her fist, connecting with her face. But her adversary was faster, striking Taya so hard, she fell backward, knocking the wind from her lungs.

The whir of a small engine carried in the distance.

Taya got to her feet, but the woman was already down the hill and running toward a four-wheeler. She climbed behind the driver whose large frame filled the seat. A dark helmet concealed his face.

They sped off into the countryside.

Keegan rushed to her side. "What're you doing?"

"She. Got. Away." Taya heaved, bracing herself with her hands flat against her knees.

"Who?"

"The passenger from the car. You didn't see her?" Taya asked, incredulous.

Keegan took her elbow, leading her back up the hill where the commotion continued.

"She was thin, slight-framed with dark hair." Taya reached up and swiped at the warmth oozing from her forehead. "That viper drew blood."

He paused and looked her over, a finger gingerly under her chin. "Yep, she got you pretty good. Probably just another of Brando's many girlfriends."

"You should see the damage I did," she joked, wincing at the throbbing pain in her temple. "Does he have female bodyguards? She's a mean fighter."

He laughed and placed a gentle kiss on her lips. "We'll get her. The important thing is Brando's in the ATF's custody."

Unconvinced, Taya argued, "She's stealthy and the four-wheeler was waiting for her."

He frowned. "Now that has me wondering. Okay, I'll ask Hawk to issue an APB. Can you can describe her enough for a composite?"

"No need, I'll draw the sketch."

"You never cease to amaze me." Keegan pulled her closer to his side.

They reached the parking lot where an ambulance had arrived. Taya spotted Folze on a stretcher.

"Is he alive?"

"Yeah, he'll pull through."

"What was that crazy renegade thing?"

"I don't know, but it helped."

Officers loaded the traffickers into cars emblazoned with Nebraska State Patrol emblems in reflective lettering. Taya followed Keegan to where two men barked orders at several officers.

Keegan approached the handsome man wearing a black tactical vest with the letters ATF printed on the front. All were equally built. The man's short dark hair was styled neatly and he had piercing blue eyes.

The second officer wore khaki pants and a gray hoodie. He turned at their approach, dismissing the officer he spoke with. His wide grin juxtaposed his intimidating stature as he pulled Keegan into a one-arm, three-pats-on-the-back man-hug. "Stryker, you knocked this one out of the park. The big dogs at HQ are gonna love you. Great job!"

Taya smiled, enjoying the exchange.

Keegan tugged her closer and faced the men. "I would've been dead without this brilliant woman. Let me introduce you both. Special Agents in Charge Otto Hawkins—" he gestured to the first man wearing the ATF vest, then addressed the second "—and Wesley Zimmer, meet Dr. Taya McGill."

Her name sounded sweet on his lips, and she appreciated his comforting proximity in the tense environment.

Wesley grabbed her hand first. "It's a pleasure to meet you."

"Thank you, sir."

"Sir? That's my pops. No, ma'am, just Wesley." He gave her a firm, friendly shake.

The first man also held out a hand. "Call me Hawk. Nice to meet you."

"Dr. McGill, I've heard great things about your work." Wesley was clearly the charmer of the two.

Taya glanced down, humbled by the words. "I'm honored."

"Thanks for joining the party." Keegan laughed.

"The party happened thanks to Wesley. He saved the day." Hawk gestured toward the active scene.

"I owe you big," Keegan agreed, slapping Wesley on the back.

"Well, in that case, I need a triple cheeseburger and fries," Wesley chuckled.

"Done." Keegan placed a hand on Taya's shoulder. "Hawk, Taya had a nasty altercation with Brando's passenger."

Hawk looked her over. "Are you all right? Let's have a medic check you out."

"No need. I'm fine. Unfortunately, she escaped on a four-wheeler in the valley. I'll compose a sketch."

"Excellent. Get it to me ASAP. What about the remains? Were you able to locate them?"

Taya nodded. She'd almost forgotten the box. "Yes, I hid them in the shelter."

"Great job. Maybe we'll recruit you for the ATF." Hawk grinned.

Wesley pointed at her motor home. "I understand the Winnebago is yours?"

Taya glanced at her Minnie Winnie, riddled with bullet holes. "Yes, sir. She's taken quite a beating."

"I'll have one of my guys confirm it's drivable while you two collect the remains." Wesley stepped away and addressed one of the officers.

Taya and Keegan took the opportunity to walk to the shelter. He didn't speak until they'd moved far enough his boss wouldn't hear them. "I've got a bone to pick with you." He cringed. "Sorry, bad choice of words."

"I'm sorry for disobeying your instructions," she said.

"Why didn't you go to the truck as I asked?"

"For the same reason you didn't wait for me before you moved into action."

"Touché. Apparently, Folze's an escape artist or I'm terrible at zip ties. Which is why I prefer old-fashioned handcuffs."

They entered the shelter and she moved to the back. "I'd love to know how he got out of the restraints." Taya reached under the tarp and gently withdrew the box, passing it to Keegan.

He cradled the container, and they returned to the Winnebago where another ATF agent tinkered under the hood. "They tried to prevent you from driving away, but we've got it fixed. We'll follow you back to Lincoln. Zimmer found plastic to cover up the rear window. It's not pretty but it'll keep the cold out for now."

"Thank you."

"Stryker, I need to speak with you before you head out," Hawk called.

Keegan faced her. "Give me a minute. I'll ride with you."

Relieved she wouldn't be returning to Lincoln with strange ATF agents, or worse, by herself, she confessed, "I was hoping you'd say that."

He jogged to his boss and Taya turned to scan the valley where Brando's passenger had disappeared on the four-wheeler.

Keegan believed they had the biggest problem solved by arresting Brando, but something told Taya the battle wasn't over.

TWELVE

Nothing killed a private conversation like a boisterous special agent in charge the size of a linebacker munching on a triple cheeseburger.

Keegan gripped the steering wheel of Taya's Minnie Winnie and glanced in the rearview mirror, making eye contact with her. He gave her another apologetic grimace, one of many since they'd left Ashfall.

Taya responded with a small grin and shrug, then shifted to the side, out of view.

She'd graciously relinquished the passenger seat to Wesley and rode in the rear of the motor home with the evidence. The time allowed Keegan and Wesley to strategize their next steps.

"I appreciate the lift." Wesley stuffed the fast-food wrapper into the bag and leaned back in the seat, stretching out his legs.

"No problem." Keegan chuckled. He'd never seen one man eat so much in such a short amount of time. "It's the least I can do considering all you did tonight."

"I had a blast. I'm sure we made record time putting that special ops plan of action together. Gave me a chance to see what's working and what's not. Without NSP's air support, we never would've got there before Brando's losers got away."

"I think I've finished the composite sketch for you." Taya leaned forward, passing a legal pad to Wesley.

He studied the paper for several minutes. "Hmm. She's familiar. I'm sure I've seen her before. Just can't place where." Lifting his phone, he snapped a picture and typed something. "I'll ask Ishi to run facial recognition."

"Who's Ishi?" Taya asked.

"The most qualified technical analyst the Feds have ever known," Wesley bragged.

"Zimmer's not exaggerating," Keegan said. "Ishi Haramoto was a black hat computer hacker in an underground organization before the ATF recruited her."

"Now, Ishi helps our agents by tapping into other worlds with her mad technical skills. The woman's a dangerous and brilliant computer genius," Wesley replied. "I'd be a mess without her."

"Has Brando fessed up?" Keegan redirected.

Wesley shook his head. "Not yet. We've got some evidence against him, but I'd love a confession. When we came down hard on Vice, he offered up everyone and everything for a plea deal. The guy's facing life in prison, but the DA might barter for a chance at parole. That's about the best he's gonna get." Wesley's phone chimed and he answered. "Yo, Ishi, whatcha got for me?"

A new appreciation for Taya's eavesdropping skills had Keegan trying to focus on the road while listening in on the call.

"Hmm. All right. Holler when you crack the mystery code. Take care of you." He disconnected.

"Good news?"

"Not yet. Ishi will be in touch. Because she's using a composite and not an actual photo, the software might take a little longer. But if she's in any database anywhere, Ishi will find her."

"Have you heard from Bear?"

Wesley twisted in his seat to address Taya. "He's doing fine. The dosage of tranquilizers Folze shot him with were more hindering than terminal. At least in Bear's case. Anyone else might've never regained consciousness."

"Bear's a force to be reckoned with," Keegan agreed.

"I know that's right." Wesley chuckled. "He's the kind of agent we should all try to emulate. The man's invincible."

"Bear's got the lives of ten cats." And they'd come too close to losing him.

A new wave of guilt invaded his thoughts. How many tragedies had he contributed to? Like a human torrential downpour of destruction, he hurt everyone he cared about.

"If you hadn't arrived when you did, he'd be a dead man for sure. Good thing you had Narcan on you." Wesley turned to Taya, his voice shifting to a professional tone. "Overdoses are rampant and law enforcement agencies require officers to keep the antidote with them at all times in case of accidental exposures."

Keegan grinned at Wesley's informative—and out of character—comment oozing with the obvious intention of impressing Taya.

"I've read about opioids like fentanyl having horrific and increased impacts on larger cities," she added.

"It's everywhere," Wesley agreed.

"How do you keep the Narcan with you while you're working undercover?"

Keegan glanced in the mirror. "I hide a dose in my boot and in my SUV."

"Did Wanda have an opioid addiction?"

His jaw clenched at the reminder. "Yes, but her drug of choice was ice."

"Methamphetamines," Wesley interpreted.

The conversation dwindled under the heavy topic.

"Would you mind if I lay down back here?" She'd probably grown bored or depressed by their talk.

"Go for it," Wesley encouraged.

Once she had moved toward the far side of the motor home, Keegan glanced in the rearview mirror. Surely, she was out of earshot, he whispered, "Give it to me straight. What kind of disciplinary action am I facing?"

"You bucked the system for sure, but your chances for the Missouri promotion are good. That is, if you're still wanting to go that route."

Keegan swallowed. "Why wouldn't I?"

Wesley shrugged. "I don't know. Maybe you'd want to stay here."

"Once the case is closed out, I have to go back to Missouri."

"Not if you took a lateral transfer."

Keegan worked the steering wheel. "There's an opening in the Omaha office?"

Wesley chuckled. "There could be. Wouldn't be an advancement, straight lateral, but you'd be in Nebraska."

Keegan's eyes flew to the rearview mirror. Had Taya overheard them? He lowered his voice, determined to change subjects. "I keep thinking about the woman Taya fought with. Why have a four-wheeler waiting to escort her from the scene?"

"If anything, you'd think Brando would've had that little insurance for himself, not a girlfriend."

"Exactly. Something doesn't make sense." He glanced in the rearview mirror again. "We need to pull out all the stops and ensure Taya's protected until we catch the woman."

"I agree. Already working with LPD and UNL Campus police." Wesley referred to the Lincoln Police Department and University of Nebraska at Lincoln where Taya's laboratory was located in Oldfather Hall. She'd process the evidence, then transfer the remains to the state patrol. They'd assume custody for the duration of the case, and at the conclusion, release Patrice for burial.

"Thanks, Wesley."

"You're not the first."

Keegan blinked. "What? You lost me."

A crooked smile formed on his friend's lips. "Don't even play like you ain't picking up what I'm putting down. You know what I'm saying. Romance happens in the field. Randee and Ace fell head over beakers for each other."

It was common knowledge in the local group that Wesley's ex-partner, ATF agent Randee Jareau, had married the scientist Ace Steele, whom she'd protected on her last case. They'd moved to Colorado after her promotion to the Denver office.

Were his feelings that obvious? He sought the appropriate response, not wanting to confirm or deny the assessment. Wesley wasn't his direct boss, but he and Hawk held the same rank. They'd talk, which might not bode well for him.

A slap to his shoulder jolted Keegan, and he gripped the wheel to recover.

"Relax. If Hawk didn't call you out on it, he ain't worried. Trust me, you won't get nothing past him." Wesley lowered his voice. "Does she know how you feel?"

Yes, and she'd shot him down. Then he'd kissed her. And she'd reciprocated. Keegan shrugged. "It's complicated."

Wesley laughed. "Man, love's always complicated."

Keegan swallowed at the *L* word. "She won't leave Nebraska." As if that one excuse justified everything.

"Hmm. And you been workin' hard for that Missouri promotion. I feel ya. Tough call." Wesley shifted in the seat. "Unless you take me up on my Omaha offer—"

"We're about thirty minutes from Lincoln," Keegan blurted.

"Roger that." Wesley stretched out. "Wake me when we get there."

Keegan focused on the blurring highway mile markers,

digesting the conversation. Would he be willing to forgo the one thing he'd sacrificed to achieve? What if he declined the promotion only to find Taya wasn't interested? She'd shot him down once. She could do it again.

Worse, if their relationship ended, he'd tanked his dreams for nothing.

Just like Taya had done with Jeremy.

Keegan sighed. No wonder she was gun-shy, afraid to make the same mistake twice. Who'd blame her? His apprehension to take a leap of faith equaled hers. He could gain true love or lose everything he'd worked for. At this stage he wasn't sure where he stood.

There are no guarantees in life. Grandma Stryker's words trailed his debate.

His work in Nebraska was ending. Once he left the state, there'd be no connection with Taya. That certain outcome scared him. Long-distance relationships weren't impossible, but he'd seen them fail too many times.

The thought of never seeing Taya again weighed like a terminal diagnosis. He couldn't pretend nothing had happened between them. But asking her if he should stay was like making her guarantee they had a future. That wasn't fair to do to her.

A cartoon soundtrack chimed from Wesley's phone, jolting the man upright. "Yo," he answered. "Uh-huh." He slapped his thigh. "I knew I'd seen her before! Get on it. You're the best, Ishi. Take care of you." He disconnected and flashed Keegan a Cheshire-cat grin.

"What?"

Movement in the back preceded Taya's approach. She leaned over the seat. "Has something happened?"

"Absolutely. Ishi identified the wild woman as Chelsea Brazownick."

Keegan paused, willing Wesley to speak faster.

"Oh, y'all never heard of her?"

"No." Keegan shook his head. "Who is she?"

"An entry-level DEA secretary."

Excitement built and Keegan's brain lined up the details. "Chelsea had access to case files. She sold off the information to Brando. We just found our mole!"

After the action-movie events Taya had endured, relief should've been her predominate emotion—except it wasn't, thanks to her eavesdropping. Wesley's example of the other ATF agent who'd married the scientist she'd protected blasted clear as tornado sirens. The veiled warning said Keegan would lose his job if they pursued a romantic relationship.

Exhaustion from the late hour, lack of sleep and days of nonstop danger weakened her feigned indifference. She'd maintained her acting skills while they'd unloaded and secured the evidence in her lab, but having others around made it easier. Standing with Keegan in her apartment proposed a new challenge. The urge to hibernate combated with her heart's cry to be near him.

"Cleared." The unfamiliar Lincoln police officer's single declaration and knowing nod preceded his exit. He descended the stairs, leaving them alone on the landing.

"Safe and sound." Keegan escorted her inside.

Taya stepped over the threshold and examined her minimalist furnishings. The latest home trends had never ranked high on her interest list, but her sparse decor brought on a fresh surge of self-consciousness. Perpendicular lines in the carpet, proof of her meticulous vacuuming, emphasized the room's spotlessness. Her beige sofa, matching recliner and overflowing bookshelf testified to a boring and sterile existence. She didn't own a TV and knickknacks meant one more thing to dust.

Taya sighed, expelling the last of her adrenaline rush

that had started to fade out somewhere on the highway between Ashfall and her laboratory.

Keegan ushered her in and closed the door behind her. "Glad to be home?"

Taya reached into her pocket and groaned. "In the chaos of moving the evidence, I forgot to grab the SIM card for us to view here."

"It'll keep for a few hours. Get some rest and we'll tackle it first thing."

Taya shook her head. "I should've stayed at the lab and finished processing the evidence."

"Why? You're already sleep deprived. Everything will wait. It's safe with *real* security in place," he added, no doubt a tongue-in-cheek reference to Folze's nonexistent security at Ashfall.

"I suppose. I just need a nap, then I'll go back in and work." She slipped out of her coat and boots.

"Let the officer downstairs know and he'll escort you. But do that after you call me." He grinned, then turned and seemed to scrutinize her belongings. Probably judging her lack of decorating skills.

She walked to the kitchen and dropped onto a chair at the breakfast bar. A strange detachment countered her normal comfort and familiarity.

Snap out of it. Her short-term role as an intricate part of a great crime fighting force was over. In reality, she was nothing more than a dull anthropologist.

Keegan crossed the room, and Taya admired his confident swagger and gorgeous exterior—the kind of man women swooned over. She'd grown accustomed to his presence and dreaded his departure.

"Now this is cool." He fingered her two-foot Charlie Brown Christmas tree with its single red ornament dangling above the small blue felt skirt.

She shrugged. "That's the extent of my holiday adornment."

"I love it, in a humorous we're-going-shopping-for-a-real-tree tomorrow sort of way." He laughed.

The promise of seeing him the next day thrilled her. Her pulse increased with each step he took closing the distance between them. Her annoying inner voice reminded her that their return to Lincoln initiated the beginning of the end. They'd secured the evidence in her laboratory, ensured officers would stand guard, refusing anyone entry, and she would begin her processing in the morning.

And with each completed task in Patrice's case, Taya would get closer to saying goodbye to Keegan. Which was best for both of them.

"We never had a chance to talk with Wesley riding along," he commented out of the blue.

"He's quite the character. I like him, and Ishi sounds fascinating," Taya directed, suddenly nervous.

"I'll introduce you to her sometime." He took her hand between his. "With all the commotion, we didn't address our kiss."

He was about to tell her how he'd made a mistake and couldn't lose his job. Taya withdrew from his touch. "Anthropologically speaking, the threat of death emphasizes the human need for physical connection. It was a purely emotional and physiological reaction. You've nothing to apologize for."

A shadow passed over Keegan's gray eyes, and he leaned closer. "If I offended you, I'm sorry, but I don't regret our kiss. However, I wanted to explain that's never happened before. Me kissing someone I was guarding."

He didn't want her to think ill or report him to his superiors. "I understand."

"And for the record, I didn't react as the result of a scientific survival response."

She looked up him, feeling his breath warm on her cheeks and swallowed. "Okay."

"I realize it's the dead of night and this isn't the time, but I wanted you to know I care for you."

What did that mean? The need to escape had Taya jumping to her feet. "Now that you mention it, I am really tired." She faked a yawn.

He nodded and stood. "Get some much deserved rest. I'd like to help with the evidence processing tomorrow."

"Will you be one of the security guards watching over me while I work?" she half joked.

"Absolutely. You and I are the ultimate team."

She yawned for real this time and covered her mouth. The power of suggestion never ceased to amaze her. "Can't argue there. Thanks again, Keegan."

Hands shoved into his jean pockets, he looked more like a nervous teenager than a robust ATF agent. Vulnerable and horribly endearing.

Stop that. They'd had a job to do and emotions were neither welcome nor appropriate. A relationship would not work. And she'd tell him so.

Tomorrow.

As if agreeing with her mental berating, Keegan said, "I'd better get going. I'll see you in the morning."

"Right."

He paused with his hand on the doorknob. "There's an officer in an unmarked car watching from the parking lot. And I'm staying at a hotel nearby. If you need anything, call. I'll be here before the cops are." He'd already told her the same thing several times, but it appeared both of them struggled with the awkward moment.

"You'd be the first I'd run to," she blurted. Heat rose up her neck, but she couldn't divert her gaze.

"I'd be crushed if you didn't." He smiled and tugged open the door. "Good night."

She locked the dead bolt; grateful he hadn't witnessed her obvious disappointment at his departure. Flipping off the light switch, she hesitated, apprehension filling her chest.

Worry for her safety wasn't the force holding Taya in place. It was the strangest realization she was alone. It seemed wrong to be without Keegan.

She shook it off. The excitement got to both of them. The kiss meant nothing. This was her real world. Her life. And it's where she belonged.

Taya turned on the small table lamp and proceeded to the bathroom.

After a long overdue and extremely hot shower, she walked to her bedroom and flipped on the strategically placed night-lights, releasing soft pinks, blues and purple glows. Snuggled under her comforter, she soaked in the calming effects, realizing she wasn't afraid of the dark. When had that happened? Had she overcome her fears after enduring the school building and cellar? Or was it an aftereffect of being with Keegan?

No. Just as Keegan had said, God helped her. She really could do all things with Him.

Still not her favorite environment, but no longer overwhelming. "Thank You, Lord."

Sleep beckoned, and she closed her eyes, surrendering to the exhaustion that had tugged at her for the past forty-eight hours. Stretching onto her side, Taya drifted off.

She jerked with the sensation of falling and glanced at the clock. Though it felt like a full night's rest, she'd only slept a short while. True to its nature, insomnia refused to give her any long-term relief.

Taya rolled to her back and stared at the ceiling, mentally rehearsing the next steps in her evidence processing. With Patrice's DNA samples already on file with the DEA, the testing would progress faster, providing a confirmation rather than an identification. And Keegan's family could lay Patrice to rest.

Keegan. Was he thinking of her, too? She glanced again at the clock. Of course not. He was asleep.

Her mind bounced around from everyday concerns to daily tasks, always returning to Keegan.

Stop that. She had no right to even allow herself to go there. Expectations bred disappointment. Keegan would get promoted and go home to Missouri. What better proof the man was a visitor than the fact that he slept in a nearby hotel?

Nebraska was home for her. She had great friends and a wonderful job.

Her sisters and their families lived on the East Coast. They were busy being a family without her, the unwanted third wheel. Never quite fitting in. Always on the outside.

What had Keegan meant when he said he cared for her? He'd been letting her down easy. That was all. Her budding attraction was ridiculous. They'd known each other a short time. She didn't believe in love at first sight. But she couldn't deny her feelings ran deeper than she cared to admit.

Her thoughts tumbled out on an imaginary conveyor belt, pushing out stacks of worries, disappointments and impossible hopes.

Another glance at the clock: 5:30 a.m.

Might as well go to the lab and work. The sooner she finished processing the evidence, the sooner Keegan would get on with his life, and she'd forget about him. He'd asked her to call if she decided to go back to the lab earlier, but she had police protection and Keegan needed rest.

Taya pushed back the covers and dressed in dark jeans and a soft ivory cowl-neck sweater. She applied a little makeup and brushed her hair. No sense in going into work looking like death warmed over. Though the real reason revolved around Keegan's arrival later on.

She grabbed her coat and pulled on a pair of brown knee-high boots. Locking up, she walked down the stairs and headed straight for the unmarked patrol car. Even if she hadn't known an officer kept watch inside, the vehicle stood out with its large side mirrors and push bumper.

The same man who'd cleared her apartment earlier that evening rolled down the window. "Ma'am, are you all right?"

"Yes, sir, I'm ready to return to the laboratory."

He sat up in the seat. "I'll let them know we're headed that way and follow you to the campus."

She contemplated arguing with him, then thought better of it and nodded. "Thanks."

Taya allowed her car to warm, flipping on the radio to silence her incessant mental debate. Christmas music filled the space with the illusion of holiday cheer. Colorful lights glowed from many of her neighbors' windows and patio railings. Taya's had none of those things.

She shifted into Drive and made the twenty-minute commute to the University of Nebraska and parked in her designated spot marked with a sign that read Anthropology Professor. Oldfather Hall was a tall brick building across from Memorial Stadium. During football season, the parking lot filled to overflowing. At this early hour, on holiday break, it sat empty.

The officer pulled up beside her and shut off his car.

Taya stepped out of the vehicle.

"I'll walk you in."

Humorless and kind of dull? Or tired and overworked? She opted for the latter and followed him down the walkway between the stadium and Oldfather Hall to a glass side entrance.

She pressed her department-issued identification badge

against the electronic reader, releasing the lock. The officer tugged open the door, and they entered, footsteps echoing in the empty building. She moved to the elevators and rode to the eighth floor. Taya glanced at the officer's name plate. Quincy.

Taya led Officer Quincy to the anthropology lab at the end of the hall where a campus officer guarded the double set of black glass doors. He stood taller at their approach.

"I'm Dr. McGill." She lifted her identification badge.

"Pleased to meet you. I'm Emmett." He barred entrance and access to the electronic security panel.

Taya hoisted her purse onto her shoulder. "Thank you both for your service. I'll take it from here."

They ignored her dismissal.

"Dr. McGill, you've got ordered protection detail," Officer Quincy replied.

"And I appreciate that very much. With you covering the elevator and stairs, I'm confident I'll be fine inside the lab. Additionally—and this is policy, not my preference—neither of you have access in the restricted area. It's not permitted. You must remain outside those doors." She pointed to the glass etched with the words Authorized Personnel.

The two officers shared a look, their expressions stiff and undeterred.

"Once I've cleared the lab, you may enter," Quincy replied. "But I'll stay with you as the evidence must have a second party witnessing at all times."

She bristled, annoyed by the inconvenience and his reminder of protocol. "Right." Taya scanned her badge, granting Quincy entrance, and waited beside Emmett.

Quincy returned and nodded his authorization. Just another reason to expedite the investigation. Having 24/7 protection was extremely invasive. She couldn't have the dynamic duo following her everywhere.

"I'll maintain watch on the elevator and stairwell doors," Emmett reassured.

"Thank you."

Taya walked to the far end of the long rectangular room. She again pressed her ID badge to the reader, releasing the lock, and entered. Her windowless corner office held two large computer monitors, a plywood desk and a small couch. Taya flipped on her desk lamp, then hung her coat and purse on the hooks behind the door. She booted her department laptop, then returned to the main area.

Taya moved to the locked evidence closet separating the wet and dry labs. She withdrew the box and envelopes for Patrice Nunes's case and placed the items on the closest of the centered five steel tables. She passed the custody log to Officer Quincy for his initials, then he relocated to a chair against the far wall facing her.

The security was overkill with Brando in custody, an APB on Chelsea and Oldfather Hall locked down with the campus police monitoring everything.

She couldn't be safer.

THIRTEEN

Taya delved into her routine, flipping on the fluorescent overhead lights and organizing her workspace. She donned her white coat and a new pair of purple surgical gloves. The familiar tasks rejuvenated her.

She distributed the box contents on the steel table, common to medical examiners and coroners. Other than his presence in her peripheral, Officer Quincy remained quiet, perched on his seat.

Taya organized the remains into the proper skeletal order, leaving space for the missing bones.

"Where are the rest?" Quincy moved beside her.

"It's unusual to find a complete skeleton in the cases like this." Taya slipped into the role of professor. "Often animals will invade the grave and make off with parts. A full skeleton isn't necessary for an identification, although it's nice to have. We use whatever we can recover."

"Bummer." He returned to his perch on the chair and withdrew his cell phone, swiping at the screen. She recognized the sounds of an app word game.

Taya examined the skull, noting a small hole where the bullet entered, but no exit wound. Most likely the cause of death, but she couldn't guarantee yet.

She gathered the three envelopes marked Evidence, containing the SIM card, bullet casing and Patrice's butter-

fly ring. She glanced at Officer Quincy, not wanting him
to view the SIM card with her. Perhaps she'd wait until
Keegan arrived. She set the envelope down and opted to
start with the ring.

Quincy continued swiping at his phone, preoccupied
with the game.

Taya walked to her microscope at the far side of the
room, withdrew the ring and set it on the glass. Peering
through the microscope, she zoomed in on the prongs of
the ring's setting.

A beep, and then a voice boomed over Officer Quincy's
radio. "I have a 10-100."

"What's a 10-100?" she asked nervously.

Quincy walked to the door. "Means he needs to use the
restroom. Excuse me a minute."

"Sure. Take your time." She peered again into the microscope, excitement building. "Well, what do we have here?"

Using a pair of tweezers, she extracted a tiny sliver of
what appeared to be dark hair. She placed the strand into
a plastic vial and set it aside. Upon further inspection, she
noticed a small rust-colored spot on the ring's surface. Taya
swabbed a sample and tested it with luminol. Sure enough,
it glowed blue.

Blood. She took a second swab of the sample and added
it to a separate vial for DNA testing.

With Quincy still absent, Taya returned to the table. She
lifted the envelope containing the SIM card. Glancing at
the double glass doors, she spotted no one and hurried to
her office. Taya propped open the door to avoid drawing
unnecessary attention when Quincy returned. She slipped
the card from the envelope and slid it into the reader connected to her laptop.

Taya inserted earbuds and replayed the entire first video
of Keegan and Skull entering Patrice's car. An involuntary
shiver coursed through her at the sight of Skull, intimi-

dating and nefarious. But her heart did a double thump at Keegan's handsome face.

Stop it.

The video was anticlimactic and ended with Patrice offering to meet them again.

Taya removed one earbud, concerned Quincy hadn't yet returned. No, his absence was better for her. She'd maximize the privacy.

She played the second footage. Again, it began with the familiar background of Patrice's car.

Taya scooted around her desk, unable to see out the door from her chair. She peeked into the lab. Still no Quincy.

Maybe he grabbed a snack on the first floor.

She hit Play and reinserted the earbud, leaning closer to the screen.

Patrice's heavily made-up face peered into the camera. Her hazel eyes gleamed behind the thick eyeliner. "Huge progress. Today is September 8 and I'm meeting with Chelsea."

Taya gasped.

Patrice continued, "She's in tight with Brando and I've worked hard to befriend her. I'm hoping she'll finally reveal his identity." She glanced up at the rearview mirror and applied a too-dark lipstick. "Showtime." She smacked her lips, then sat back.

Within a few minutes, the passenger door opened and the same woman Taya battled entered. "Hey, Butterfly."

"Chelsea, are you okay?" Patrice's tone was soft.

The woman's right eye was black and blue and she had a small cut above her lip. "Yeah, no big deal."

"What happened? Did Brando do that to you?"

Chelsea grimaced and her lip quivered. "He got angry when I asked him to meet you. He's getting anxious. Says the Feds are onto him."

"Do you think that's true?" Patrice glimpsed at the camera.

Chelsea shrugged. "Who knows? He's so paranoid. Maybe it's for the best."

"You could turn him in. The cops would see that as a good thing and you wouldn't get in trouble, too."

"I can't do that to Brando! No way." Chelsea's eyes filled with tears. "I love him."

"How long are you going to live this way?" Patrice laid her hand on Chelsea's shoulders. "He'll kill you."

"I ain't leavin'. Where else would I go? Brando takes care of me."

"Abuse isn't love, and it's not taking care of you. You could go to a shelter."

Chelsea laughed bitterly. "And what? Hide out until they kick me to the curb? This is my life, Butterfly. But you wouldn't understand."

"Why wouldn't I?"

"Because you've never been homeless. When a man wants to take care of you, you stick by him. Loyalty. That's what the group is about."

"I understand loyalty to the people you love." Patrice sighed and reached into her purse, retrieving a tissue. She passed it to Chelsea.

"If Brando found out… No, it's too risky." The woman fidgeted.

Several moments passed. Patrice glanced at the camera. "I need to tell you something. A secret. I'll help you get away."

Taya's hand flew to her mouth. *Don't tell her!*

Chelsea sniffled. "How?"

Patrice blew out a long breath. "You'd have to tell me who Brando is. His real identity."

Chelsea shook her head, her long hair sweeping back and forth in vehement disagreement. "No. I can't. He trusts me."

"I trust you enough to tell you my secret."

The woman's large eyes blinked at Patrice. "Why would you do that?"

"Because I care what happens to you. You're my friend."

Chelsea swiped at her nose and nodded. "Okay."

Taya gripped the sides of the laptop, as if doing so would stop Patrice from speaking the dreaded words.

"I'm not who you think I am. I'm a DEA agent."

"You are?" Chelsea's eyes grew wide. "You're the Fed?"

"Yes. But we'll help each other."

Taya listened in horrified silence as Patrice revealed her undercover status to Chelsea, promising to keep her out of jail if she turned on Brando. They agreed to meet again the next evening and Chelsea left.

Alone again, Patrice shut off the camera without a word.

Taya reached into her purse for her cell, realizing she didn't have one anymore. Swiveling in her chair, she grabbed the desk phone and dialed Keegan's hotel. The phone rang four times before a clerk answered.

Which room was he in? "I need the room for Keegan Stryker."

"What room number?" The clerk's boredom oozed through the line.

"I don't know."

"Ma'am, I'm sorry but without—"

"This is an emergency! Find him. Now!" Taya slammed her hand on the desk.

The sound of keyboard clicks. "Please hold."

At last the line rang again.

"Hello," Keegan croaked, his voice deeper and raspier.

"It's Taya."

"What's wrong?"

"I couldn't sleep and came into work. I've watched the second video." She rattled off the details, explaining how Patrice promised to help Chelsea if she turned on Brando.

"Keegan, Chelsea must've turned on Patrice and got her killed."

A pop echoed from the lab. Taya froze, eyes fixed on her open office door. She tried to stretch, but the desk phone cord leashed her, restricting movement.

"Keegan. Wait. I just heard something, hold on," she whispered.

"Taya, don't—"

She set down the receiver and rounded her desk.

The overhead lights went out, plunging her into darkness. Taya spun on her heel and reached across for the phone. A slam to the back of her head flattened her on the desktop. She placed both hands on the surface and pushed herself up. Another hit to the side of her head sent her stumbling into the wall.

"I gave you chances. Told Folze to encourage you to leave for Christmas. All you had to do was leave for one stupid night." A familiar voice.

Only the soft glow of her desk lamp and computer filled the room.

Taya braced herself and turned. "Chelsea. How did you get in here?" She raised her voice, hoping Keegan heard her. "Where's Officer Quincy?"

"He's indisposed." Chelsea chuckled.

"What about the campus security officer, Emmett? They'll be coming."

The slender woman blocked the exit, gripping a pistol. Her dark eyes narrowed and a reptilian smile creased her face. "Emmett? Oh, he's doing great. The reason I'm here after all. For a smart doctor, you aren't very perceptive."

Keep her talking. Taya focused on Chelsea, determined not to draw her attention to the laptop or the receiver on her desk. "Why do you say that?"

"I told Emmett it was too much of a risk for him to be your 'security guard.'" Chelsea made one-handed air quotes on the last words. "I can't believe you didn't recognize him from his daring rescue on the four-wheeler." She rolled her eyes and tsked. "Too bad. If you'd paid better attention, you could've warned poor Officer Quincy."

Taya swallowed. "Please, Chelsea, you don't want to do this. The authorities are searching for you. Turn yourself in, tell them how Brando used you, and they'll grant you leniency. You don't deserve to pay for his misdeeds."

The woman cackled and raised the gun higher. "All that academic knowledge has eliminated your common sense. You are stupid. So sad your boyfriend isn't here to protect you this time." Her tone shifted, growing cold and indifferent.

A chill crept down Taya's spine.

"Yes, you will die. It's the only way."

Keegan had shot out of the bed at Taya's call. As soon as Chelsea's voice came across the line, he'd grabbed his jeans off the chair. The short hotel phone cord entangled him, and he fought to keep the receiver pressed tightly against his ear while grabbing his keys.

Horrified, he listened to the exchange between Taya and Chelsea. How had Brando's girlfriend gotten into the lab?

No response or sign she'd lifted the receiver again. If he called out and Chelsea heard him, she'd hang up the phone. Maybe she wasn't aware Taya had been talking to him.

His cell rang. Keegan tucked the hotel receiver against his left ear and stretched to reach his phone with his right hand. He glanced at the screen before answering. Wanda.

"She'll-kill'er," Wanda slurred.

"I'll call you back." Keegan strained to hear Taya's side of the conversation.

"Brando will kill her." Wanda enunciated the words slower.

"Brando's in jail. He's not killing anyone," Keegan replied, patience evaporating.

"No, no." She wheezed. "Lance is in jail. Brando doesn't care."

Keegan's attention shifted. "Wanda. What're you saying?"

"Brando."

He had to help Taya, and Wanda's words made no sense. "I had to do it."

Great. Of all the times in the world for Wanda to lose it and start tweaking again, she chose this moment to call.

"Wanda, I'll call you back."

He disconnected and dialed Hawk with one hand.

"I'm an early riser, Stryker, but this is ridiculous."

"Hawk, get units to UNL now!" Keegan launched into a quick explanation.

"I'll meet you there." He hung up.

Keegan didn't want to let go of the connection he had with Taya, but he had to release the hotel receiver. He set it on the bed, not wanting to hang up and alert Chelsea when the line disconnected.

Please, God, help her.

He sprinted from the room, down the hallway and into the stairwell. He blasted through the lobby doors and bolted for his car.

He drove straight to UNL. Thankfully, the early hour meant minimal traffic, but Keegan struggled to stay within the speed limit. Whipping into the parking lot, his gaze traveled to the familiar unmarked cruiser devoid of Officer Quincy. He slammed into Park, lunged out and jogged toward the building.

No light from the overhead streetlamps illuminated the walkway between Memorial Stadium and Oldfather Hall. Keegan glanced up. The broken bulbs conveyed a purposeful move. Gun in hand, he proceeded with caution. He didn't have to walk far before confirming his apprehension.

A pair of men's boots peeked from beneath a bush near the anthropology building's outer doors. Keegan rushed to where the Lincoln PD officer man lay.

Keegan pressed his fingers against the officer's neck and sighed relief at the strong pulse.

He groaned and Keegan helped him sit up. "What happened?"

"Not sure." He put a hand against his head. "Got smacked on the head and everything went black. Where's Dr. McGill?"

Anger rose, panic on its heels.

"Where did you last see her?"

"In her lab."

"Help is on the way." Keegan clutched his nine-millimeter tighter and hurried to Oldfather Hall. Where were Hawk and his backup?

He tugged on the door, surprised at the ease with which it opened. The access to the building should've been locked.

The hairs on the back of his neck rose, and he glanced up. The security cameras were in place overhead, but instinct said they wouldn't help him tonight.

He ran to the elevator and pressed the button, but no light illuminated. Keegan ran for the stairwell. The door opened a few inches, butting against something.

Keegan shoved all his weight against the metal, creating a space big enough to squeeze through. His foot slid on the wet linoleum, and he grasped the door for balance. He stepped backward and stumbled over the obstacle that had hindered his entrance.

A campus officer lay sprawled facedown. Once more, Keegan checked for a pulse. The man was alive but out for the count.

Keegan sprinted up the next flight, taking two and three steps at a time. He reached the landing for the seventh floor and rounded the corner.

A slam to his chest thrust him backward and he tumbled down the stairs. His nine-millimeter bounced through the railing and plummeted to the bottom. Keegan grasped the handrail and jerked himself upright. He backed against the wall on the sixth-floor landing.

Footsteps approached and a second campus officer stood above, staring down at him. The barrel of his gun grew to the size of a cannon, aimed at Keegan.

The officer grinned and hefted the pistol higher. Finger poised on the trigger.

The door behind the man opened. "Good job," the officer said. "Wanda, come on out."

Keegan shifted to the side as the familiar scraggly blond emerged. "You're alive?"

She ignored him, focused on the officer. "Emmett, can I see Molly?"

Keegan's mind raced. Wanda's daughter had been in the system for over a year and with Wanda's priors, current parole and drug rehab program still in the works, she didn't meet the requirements to regain custody of her baby. Had this jerk used that to trip her up?

Emmett chortled. "No, stupid. You ain't never gettin' your brat. You're a worthless mess."

Something flickered in her eyes and she fisted her hands.

"Wanda. Where's Dr. McGill?" Keegan purposefully used her title. If this imbecile thought he had feelings for Taya, he'd use it as a weapon.

"With Brando," Wanda whimpered.

A blast echoed from above. Emmett turned at the noise, and Keegan launched himself at him, tackling Emmett into the door.

They shifted and rolled down the stairs, slamming onto the landing with such force Keegan's teeth rattled.

He punched Emmett in the stomach. Emmett returned a hit to Keegan's ribs, but adrenaline masked the pain.

Rolling himself over Emmett, he grabbed the man's hand to force the gun from his grip. Knee digging into Emmett's chest, Keegan banged his hand against the stair. He repeated the move twice until the pistol bounced free. The men wrestled as Keegan fought Emmett from recovering his weapon.

"Wanda, grab the gun!" Keegan ordered.

In his peripheral, she moved, but Keegan was busy battling Emmett. Several gut punches nearly had him puking.

Keegan beat his fist into Emmett's smug face, but it was like hitting concrete. He tried again, hand throbbing. Unrelenting, Keegan thrust an elbow, connecting with the man's nose. A satisfying crunch preceded a holler of pain.

Jumping to his feet, a blast sent Keegan jerking back. A dark stain grew on Emmett's white uniform and he stilled.

Keegan turned.

Wanda clutched the pistol with both hands. Determination etched in her expression. "He lied about Molly." Her eyes darted wildly from Emmett to Keegan.

"Wanda, put down the gun. You're safe now," he assured her, inching closer.

She nodded and dropped the weapon.

"Stay here, okay?"

She stared at the dead man.

"He won't hurt you anymore," Keegan said. "Help is coming."

Wanda dropped to a squat, hugging herself. She rocked back and forth, and Keegan recognized the lullaby she hummed.

He snatched up the pistol, grabbed Emmett's campus identification badge from his uniform and bolted up the stairs to the eighth floor, praying he wasn't too late.

Keegan thrust open the stairwell door and sprinted down the hallway to the laboratory.

The double set of black glass doors were closed, but he

spotted Taya inside. Chelsea's arm was wrapped around her throat in a stranglehold, gun against her head.

Keegan pressed the ID against the electronic lock and the doors whooshed open. Gun gripped tightly and aimed at Chelsea, he entered the lab.

"Don't come any closer," Chelsea screeched, pushing the muzzle harder against Taya's temple.

"Chelsea, you don't want to hurt Dr. McGill." Fear tightened his throat.

The woman lifted an eyebrow. "How do you know my name?"

"You work for the DEA, right?" Keegan inched toward her.

"Where's Wanda?" Her eyes darted to the doors.

"She's with Emmett. It's over, Chelsea. Let Dr. McGill go."

"Take another step and I'll put a bullet into her brain." She pushed the gun harder against Taya's temple, eliciting a wince. "Where's Emmett?"

"He's dead. I know a lot about you. How Lance called himself Brando and then used you."

She laughed.

"Cops are swarming this place," he said, praying it was true. "Let Dr. McGill go. She's got nothing to do with what you want."

"She's got everything! If she'd stayed away, she wouldn't have to die," Chelsea countered.

"Chelsea, you're in control," he said soothingly, using his negotiating skills. "Let her go and tell me what you want. I'll make it happen."

"Right, like I believe a cop."

"Brando hurt you," Taya croaked over Chelsea's throat grip. "Let Agent Stryker help you."

"Lance's in custody. You're safe now. I'll help you," Keegan bargained, watching Chelsea's expression.

"You're both so gullible. Just like that dumb DEA agent."

Keegan clenched his jaw, shoving down his emotions. Wanda had said Taya was with Brando. He studied the woman again and the realization smacked him. "Chelsea, I know you're Brando."

Her eyes widened. "Did Lance tell you? He promised to take the fall! He promised to take care of me!"

"Wait. She's Brando?" Taya asked.

"Shut up!" Chelsea backed against the large windows. She had nowhere to go. A tiny red light appeared through the glass, reflecting off Chelsea's shoulder.

Thank You, Lord. His team had arrived. He kept his gaze on Chelsea's face, not wanting to draw attention to the police sniper's target on her shirt.

"Put down your gun or I'll shoot her." Chelsea's hand shook slightly.

He couldn't risk her hand accidentally pulling the trigger. Keegan hesitated. If the sniper missed, he'd have no way to protect Taya.

"Do it!" Chelsea shrieked.

"Okay. I'm setting down my gun." He locked eyes with Taya. *Please, Lord, help her remember my instructions from earlier.* "Taya, do you trust me?"

She attempted to nod, but Chelsea's stranglehold restricted her movement.

"You're wasting your time," Chelsea warned.

Keegan didn't move his gaze from Taya. "Whatever happens, Taya McGill, listen to me. You can't *drop dead* on me. I need you."

"Yeah, yeah, she gets it. You need her. Put down your gun!"

Keegan knelt and set down his nine-millimeter. "You hear me?" he said louder, still squatting. "Taya, you cannot *drop dead*!"

Her eyes widened in understanding and her body went limp, sliding through Chelsea's grasp.

A blast shattered the window, raining glass.

Chelsea screamed from the impaling bullet wound. Grip tight on her gun, she reflexively fired a shot into the ceiling before losing her grip. The gun toppled to the floor. She spewed a long string of curse words and useless threats. She clutched her arm, blood seeping through her olive-green jacket. Taya swept Chelsea's legs, forcing her to the ground.

Keegan dove, slamming into Chelsea, forcing her face-down.

Bright light and a thundering explosion invaded the lab. The flash-bang preceded the ATF team's entrance through the smoke.

"Get down. Get down!"

Ears ringing and vision blurred by the smoke, Keegan struggled to handcuff Chelsea as she wriggled and kicked like a three-year-old. Hauling her to her feet, he passed Chelsea to a familiar agent and moved to where Taya stood, holding on to a steel table. She swiped at her eyes and relief covered her face.

Keegan pulled her into his arms, not caring who saw them. "Are you okay?"

Taya nodded against his chest, then clung to him. Her shoulders heaved. He glanced down, heart wrenching at her tears, and fear eked through him. "What happened? Were you hit?" He leaned down, examining her for injuries.

Taya released her death grip and took a small step back. "Sorry, I guess it came at me all at once."

Relieved, he embraced her again. "Don't apologize. You've been through the wringer. I'm so proud of you. Your timing was perfect."

"I should've stayed in bed," Taya half joked.

Chelsea's string of expletives carried across the room, increasing in volume and vulgarity. "You'll pay! You're all gonna pay," she shrieked as the agent dragged her into the hallway.

Wesley approached, glancing over his shoulder. "Ooooh, she's got a mouth on her. Gonna have to disinfect my ears after that little interaction."

Keegan laughed. "Yeah, my grandmother would've had a fit."

Wesley's dark eyes moved to Taya, and concern etched the big man's forehead. "Dr. McGill, are you all right?"

"Yes." She straightened her shoulders and addressed Keegan. "How'd you know they'd shoot Chelsea when they did?"

"Sniper light," Wesley interjected.

"You were the sniper?" Keegan asked, incredulous.

"You betcha." Wesley smiled wide. "What? You didn't think a talented sniper could look this good?"

Taya laughed.

"Chelsea won't be bowling anytime soon, but I wanted to make sure she'd stand trial. Wish we'd had audio up in here." Wesley faced Taya. "Your timing was impeccable. How'd you slip free of her hold?"

She turned to Keegan. "I just did what he told me to."

He winked at her and caught a knowing grin from Wesley.

"Wish some of my men followed orders that well," Wesley said.

Taya shivered and Keegan looked down. "What's wrong?"

"Just leftover adrenaline," she assured him, lifting her hand. She held it up to the light, then spun and scurried to a table where the remains were splayed out.

Keegan shot a look at Wesley and they followed Taya.

She removed a few strands of hair caught in her fingers and slipped them into an evidence bag.

"What's going on?" Keegan asked.

Taya ignored him and slipped on a pair of latex gloves, then grabbed two cotton swabs. She scurried to swipe a spot of blood spatter on the floor and placed them in plastic vials for testing. Last, she reached for the casing from Chelsea's gun that had landed behind a table leg.

Hawk entered the room and walked to Keegan, confusion in his expression as Taya worked. "Emmett's DOA, Wanda's in custody. She's pretty shook up. Won't tell us anything and keeps asking to speak to you, Stryker."

"I'd better go talk to her."

"Dr. McGill," Hawk began, "we have forensic technicians who'll gather—"

"No need. Thanks to Chelsea's attack, she left evidence behind. She just made my job a hundred times easier. I'll use her hair and blood to test against the evidence I found earlier in Patrice's ring."

Keegan did a double take. "What? When did that happen?"

Hawk and Wesley stared at her, obviously lost in the conversation.

"Dr. McGill, please start from the beginning." Hawk spoke first.

Taya launched into the story from her call out to the grave site through the events that concluded with viewing the videos in her office before Chelsea attacked her.

Hawk jerked to look at Keegan. "Were you aware of these things?"

"Yes, sir." Anticipating disciplinary action, Keegan didn't elaborate.

"We'll discuss it later," Hawk said.

Wesley slapped a hand on Keegan's shoulder, clearly picking up on Hawk's less than thrilled response. "Aw, man, from what I understand, y'all been on the run from the get-go. I'm sure Stryker had full intention to disclose all of this first thing in the morning."

"It is first thing in the morning," Hawk countered.

Taya thankfully interrupted before the conversation heated up anymore. "When I inspected the ring under the microscope, I discovered a sliver of hair caught between the prongs and a discoloration that tested positive for blood."

"Outstanding!" Wesley said.

"Unfortunately, that won't prove who the killer was," Hawk said.

"Nah, but if Chelsea's DNA matches, it proves she was near Patrice when she was killed," Keegan argued.

Taya grinned and lifted the casing she'd picked up from the floor moments before. She reached over and grabbed the evidence bag containing the casing she'd taken from the grave at Ashfall. "Even better, if these casings match, you'll have your smoking gun."

Keegan walked to retrieve Chelsea's gun from where the arresting officer had placed it. "We can hope she used the same weapon. Looks like she prefers this one. Even has her name engraved in the side."

"Let's take a look at those videos," Wesley suggested.

Taya led them back to her office and played the footage on her laptop.

Keegan shook his head, forehead creased. "Chelsea's job at the DEA office didn't allow her access to the undercover information, but once Patrice identified herself, it would've been easy for her to follow up."

"When Chelsea learned Patrice was an undercover agent, she killed her—" Wesley said.

"—or had her killed," Hawk interrupted.

"Then Folze buried her," Taya concluded.

Keegan nodded. "Chelsea had opportunity to start the rumors about Patrice to throw off the investigation. Even plant false evidence. But the one thing that didn't make sense was Wanda's rambling about Brando."

Hawk quirked a brow. "We have Brando in custody."

"Not according to Wanda. She said Brando had Taya."

"Chelsea is Brando," Taya said.

"Whoa. No way," Hawk replied.

"I'd better talk to Wanda before they take her in." Keegan spun on his heel and walked out of the laboratory.

"Go ahead, I'll take Dr. McGill's statement," Hawk said from behind him.

The beseeching look Taya shot him almost had Keegan reconsidering, but a nagging sensation said Wanda would confirm the conclusion of the Brando puzzle.

FOURTEEN

Keegan closed the distance to where Wanda sat shrinking into a chair as an officer dragged Chelsea through the hallway.

"You stupid cow! You better not tell them anything! You hear me? Or you're never going to see your kid! Not ever!" Chelsea's threats ended with a thud of the stairwell door.

Wanda glanced up at his approach.

Keegan recognized the young agent standing guard but couldn't remember his name. "Can I have a few minutes to talk with her?" The question was more of a professional courtesy than a request for permission.

The man nodded and quietly stepped away.

Wanda's wrists were handcuffed behind her back. Frail and eyes red-rimmed, she looked more like a scared child than a grown woman.

Keegan knelt beside her. "Don't listen to a word she says, Chelsea's just trying to scare you."

"Doesn't matter. I'm going to jail again." Wanda looked down.

He swallowed hard, not wanting to give her false hope. "I'll tell the judge all you've done to help me."

"Thanks, Keegan." She bit her lip. "I'm sorry. Emmett threatened to hurt Molly if I didn't do what he said. But I didn't hurt those other cops."

"I'm guessing he used you as a distraction and attacked them?"

She nodded. "He stole the badge off a campus security officer to get into the building."

Disdain for the creep filled Keegan again. But Wanda had to take responsibility for her actions, regardless of the threats. "You'll have to tell the officer who takes your statement every single detail. Do you understand?"

"Yeah."

"I appreciate everything you did. You saved my life. Twice."

She shrugged.

"What's Chelsea afraid you're going to say?"

Wanda shook her head.

"She's not here so she can't hear you," Keegan assured.

"Will she go to jail?"

"For a very long time. She tried to kill Dr. McGill. But she's done more than that, hasn't she?"

Wanda sighed. "If I say anything, she'll kill me."

"She won't have the opportunity. I'll be sure the DA is aware of how hard you've worked for the ATF. I'll request protection for you and ask for them to keep you in separate facilities." A weak offer at best, but it was all he could do at the moment. Depending on how much information Wanda provided, the DA might work out a deal with her. But it would have to be substantial. "We have Lance in custody—"

"Lance isn't Brando," Wanda whispered. "That's what Chelsea doesn't want me to tell you. Lance is her boyfriend." Wanda shifted in the seat. "He's not a bad guy. He's always been nice to me."

Everything in Keegan wanted to refute her concept of a *bad guy*. Instead, he listened.

Wanda continued to look down and spoke softly. "Lance does whatever Chelsea tells him to do. She uses him like she does everyone. She always gets what she wants. Always has. No matter what it costs. Even if she hurts the other person." Wanda's lip trembled. "I'm tired of being used."

Keegan rested his hand on her bony shoulder. "Let's work together then and stop Chelsea so she can't do that anymore to anyone." And he felt guilty for falling into that category. "How do you know all of this about her?"

"Because sisters share secrets."

Keegan blinked, the information seeping into his brain at sloth speed. "Chelsea's your sister?"

"Yes." She looked up and shrugged. "We got different daddies, but the same momma. She says I embarrass her so I'm not supposed to tell anyone."

"Why—" He didn't finish the question.

The floodgates opened and Wanda rambled on. "I should've told you, but Chelsea promised to help me get Molly back if I kept her secret. She said we'd be rich and I could take Molly far away from here. All I ever wanted was my baby. I'd do anything for her. I've been trying so hard to stay clean, even when Chelsea offered me the drugs. Telling me it would numb the pain." She met his eyes, and behind the dark circles, he saw her broken mother's heart.

He squelched his frustration and swallowed, unsure where to start the million questions tackling his mind.

"Lance is the only one who ever told me the truth. He said Chelsea was keeping me from Molly." A tear streaked her face. "I'm real sorry, Agent Stryker. You been good to me. I'm sorry for messin' up again."

He pulled her into a side hug, afraid her frail frame would snap under his touch. "You saved my and Dr. McGill's lives." He released her and squatted again.

Wanda's gaze shifted to the closed stairwell door as if she expected it to burst open.

"Talk to me," Keegan pressed.

She met his eyes and nodded. "Chelsea is really Brando."

Though he knew the information, Keegan wanted every detail. "Chelsea manipulated Lance into pretending to be Brando so he'd go to jail instead of her?"

"Yes. But Lance don't deserve that. He ain't done nothing."

That was debatable. "Will he testify against her?"

Wanda shrugged. "Maybe? If not, I will. What else do I have to lose?"

"Agent Stryker, we need to go," interrupted the arresting officer, coming back into the room.

Keegan helped Wanda to her feet. "Thank you."

Excitement coursing through him, Keegan rushed back to the lab where Hawk, Taya and Wesley stood talking.

Unable to contain the information he blurted, "Wanda confirmed it, Chelsea is Brando. And it gets better, Wanda and Chelsea are half sisters. She just filled in the missing pieces."

"Chelsea is the nefarious mastermind behind a huge trafficking cartel? I did not see that coming." Wesley shook his head.

"Chelsea knew Molly was a carrot she could dangle to keep Wanda in line."

"So why suddenly tell us the truth?" Hawk asked.

"Lance told Wanda she wouldn't get Molly back, but it was like the bulb went on in her head and she unleashed her anger when Emmett said the same thing."

Taya leaned against the table. "Chelsea manipulated her own sister? How cruel to lure Wanda with the promise of getting her parental rights returned! She controlled her with that glimmer of hope, knowing full well Wanda would do anything to get Molly—"

"Except get off drugs and clean up her life," Hawk interrupted.

Taya visibly bristled. "Addiction is an illness," she argued, then turned her attention to Keegan. "But I don't understand. How did Chelsea know Wanda was your CI?"

"More than likely she didn't at first. But once she found out, she could maximize that knowledge to her advantage. And getting me to doubt my own team was a perfect tactic. A house divided cannot stand," Keegan quoted.

"Chelsea's a narcissist. She used Lance as her cover, ensuring he would take the fall if she was arrested. She had Wanda playing games. Man, talk about a criminal genius." Wesley tsked.

"Why would Lance give up Chelsea now?" Hawk asked.

"If he cares for Wanda like she said, he'll talk," Keegan inserted.

"Let's hope Lance grows a backbone for Wanda's sake. And when he realizes the charges he's facing," Wesley interjected.

"We've got our work cut out for us. I'll start by sending Chelsea's gun and the one found at Skull's scene off to ballistics ASAP," Hawk said.

"Once this is finished, Patrice deserves a proper burial with full honors," Keegan said. "I want her name officially cleared and her reputation restored."

Hawk nodded. "I'll do my best. But we're taking the word of a known drug user. If Gunner Folze's testimony corroborates Wanda's, it'll add credence, but we'll still need hard evidence."

"I have a feeling Folze will gladly do anything to help reduce his sentence," Taya said. "The man is as wishy-washy as a wet noodle and in the meantime—" she gestured toward the table "—Patrice will tell us everything we need."

Hawk nodded. "Dr. McGill, your reputation precedes you. I have full confidence your findings will be the catalyst to ensure justice for Agent Nunes." He turned to Keegan. "Selfishly speaking, I hate to lose you, but HQ will be elated. I'm sure the Missouri promotion is right around the corner."

Keegan cleared his throat. "Actually, Hawk, that's something I need to talk to you about."

Taya jerked to look at him and her smile faded. She busied herself with the evidence envelopes. "I'll start working on these," she said, excusing herself and hurried to her office.

Wesley grinned wide and mouthed, *Omaha*, before walking out.

Hawk focused on Keegan. "What was that all about?"

This was it. "I'm passing on the promotion."

Hawk glanced to where Taya had disappeared into her office. "Stryker, you need to reconsider. I've always encouraged my team to better themselves and move up the ladder. Why would you want to miss out on the chance of a lifetime?"

Keegan shrugged. "Something else will come along." No. *Someone* else had already come along, and he wasn't about to let her go. Even if there was no guarantee she felt the same way.

"Wesley mentioned the option of an Omaha lateral position?" Hawk sighed.

"He did."

"Remind me to have a talk with him about recruiting my people," Hawk grumbled with a good-natured grin. "I hate to lose you. You're heads above the rest as far as I'm concerned. But I understand. Taya seems like a great lady."

"Hawk, let's go take care of cleanup," Wesley called from the doorway.

Hawk slapped Keegan on the shoulder. The two SACs were the last to leave the room, and Keegan waited until the glass doors closed before walking to Taya's office.

He paused at the entrance until she looked up. "Everyone's finally gone. So, Dr. McGill, we have a few things to address. May I come in?"

A shimmer in her eyes drove an edge of confusion through him. She blinked back the tears and her confident air returned. "Has your team completed their procedures?"

"I'm sure they're close to finished." He dropped onto the chair opposite her desk.

She steepled her fingers. "I'd like to begin compiling the evidence as soon as possible. We should have results within a few days."

"Excellent." He tilted his head. Why the sudden cold shoulder and icy professionalism?

"When will you return to Missouri?"

So that was what was wrong. She figured he was leaving. "I'm not sure. It'll depend on a few things."

Taya's eyebrows peaked. "I see. You told your boss about the kiss?"

"Of course not."

She glanced down, shuffling papers on the desk. "Oh. Well, good. There's no need to mention it. I certainly won't say anything. It doesn't behoove either of us and taints our professional statuses."

And now he was thoroughly confused. "I'm sorry, but you've totally lost me."

"I overheard you and Wesley talking on the way back from Lincoln."

He swallowed. He'd underestimated her eavesdropping skills in the motor home. How much had she heard? "Okay."

"Keegan, I'd never jeopardize your career." Her eyes seemed to search him. "The kiss was a onetime thing. Nothing worth losing your job over."

He held up a hand. "Whoa. Say what? Why would I lose my job?"

Taya looked down. "Wesley said the other agent had

to move away because she became romantically involved with her charge."

Keegan chuckled. "Dr. McGill, I'm afraid your hypothesizing has speared off in the wrong direction."

"I beg your pardon?" She narrowed her gaze.

He sat back and placed an ankle over his opposite knee. "The agent Wesley mentioned, Randee Jareau, moved because she was promoted to the Denver office. She wasn't fired for falling in love."

Taya blinked. "She wasn't?"

"No." Keegan stood and rounded the desk, sitting on the surface. He took Taya's hands into his.

"So, it's okay that we kissed?"

He leaned in closer. "Absolutely. Unless you feel otherwise?"

Her dark eyelashes fluttered low, and a blush crept across her cheeks. "I never said that. But what about your job? You have to return to Missouri."

"Actually, I don't. Wesley offered me a lateral position to stay and work for him in the Omaha office."

She bit her lower lip, drawing his attention there. "You'd turn down the promotion and move to Nebraska?"

"Yes. To be near you."

"Why would you do that?"

Heart thundering in his chest, he plunged on. Better to find out now if she wasn't interested. Not that he'd give up. It just meant figuring out how hard he'd have to work to win her affections. "I'm fully aware of how ludicrous this might sound to you. We've spent all our time running from criminals. Let me get this out before I lose my nerve."

"Okay." She tilted her head.

"Remember when we talked about fears?"

She nodded.

"My fear is relationships. They scare me more than clowns and horror films."

"A fear of relationships can be attributed to several other phobias. Though it might depend on the specific kind. For instance, the fear of clowns in general is called coulrophobia—"

"Taya!"

She bit her lip and focused on him.

"Let's try this again. Losing Patrice and being with you, all of it has made me see what I want more than my job. Or a promotion. Those things are great now, but someday it'll just be me. And that's not appealing."

Taya didn't respond.

Man, she made this tough. "I'm falling for you. Hard. Like roller-coaster loop-de-loop hard. If you'll allow me, I'd like to explore our relationship."

She blinked and for a moment he worried she'd run screaming from the office. Except he still held her hands.

"Did you hear me?"

"You want to date me?"

"Sort of. I don't believe in dating as a hobby. If we're seeing each other, it's aiming toward something real. A future together."

"You can't give up your dreams for someone like me," she squeaked, lips quivering.

Keegan leaned closer. "What?"

Taya averted her gaze and withdrew from his touch. "Keegan, you're amazing. And kind. And gorgeous. We're in different leagues."

"Hey, look at me."

She didn't move, and he gently placed a finger under her chin, lifting her head to face him. "You're the most beautiful, brilliant, exciting woman I've ever met. I'm not giving up anything. If you'll have me, I'll be gaining everything I've ever wanted. In you."

"Really?"

"Absolutely." He helped her to stand and pulled her

closer. "I realize your disdain for LEOs, but maybe you'd make an exception. Just this once?"

She chuckled. "I may have had a change of heart in that regard."

"I don't mean to question your judgment, and for the record, I'm in favor of such a decision, but what changed your mind?"

"You've chipped at my unreasonableness. But when Chelsea held me hostage, it hit me. You asked if I trusted you and I didn't have to think about it. I knew. I trust you with all my heart. I'd even be willing to walk away from all of this." She gestured wide.

He slid his hands to her waist, and she reciprocated by wrapping her arms around his neck.

She combed her fingers through his hair, sending shivers down his spine, drinking him in with her eyes. Apprehension and tenderness danced in her blue irises.

"I love you, Taya McGill." He watched, praying she didn't pull away.

She leaned closer. "I love you, too."

"I have the best Christmas gift ever."

She melted against him, and Keegan swept his lips over hers, tender, questioning. Extending the challenge.

She deepened the kiss. Challenge accepted.

EPILOGUE

One week before Christmas, a year later

Taya lifted the string of blue tree lights and hummed along to the familiar carol playing softly from the speaker. She relished the sight of her handsome husband decked out in his favorite yellow hoodie and jeans, squatting beside the ridiculous amount of decorations.

"Most people don't get married, move cross-country and decorate for Christmas all in their honeymoon period," she said, untangling the mass.

"Ah, but we're way more adventurous than the average newlyweds," Keegan contended with a teasing grin.

They'd agreed the promotion to the ATF Joint Task Force in Quantico qualified as the perfect wedding gift, other than the annoying and intrusive timing.

"Are you sure you bought two sets?" Keegan asked.

She trusted the gorgeous man to take down bad guys, evade vehicle-pursuing psychos and be her protector, but locating a strand of Christmas lights appeared to be his undoing.

Taya smothered a giggle, spotting the package immediately, and contemplated how long to torture him with the search.

"I'm telling you, they're not here," he grumbled, digging through the mess. A snort escaped her lips and Keegan looked up. "What?"

"Under the garland by your left hand." She released the giggle.

He glanced down, lifted the set and groaned. With feigned triumph, he exclaimed, "Aha."

Together, they worked to set the lights on the twelve-foot artificial tree. Keegan treated the massive greenery like a mountain to be conquered with an overabundance of tinsel and ornaments.

"Perhaps we should've started with a smaller tree?" she asked for the tenth time.

"Pah! You've missed way too many Christmases so we've got a lot of making up to do. Besides, big trees are a Stryker family tradition. It's our duty, on our first Christmas as a married couple, to establish a baseline for future decorating expectations."

Taya grinned at his reasoning but didn't argue. Truthfully, she was grateful for the enthusiasm he brought. "I'd take this any day over what we endured a year ago."

Wanda had supervised visitations with Molly and had almost finished her court-appointed rehab. While Chelsea faced life in prison.

Keegan swept her into his arms and lowered his head. "Just so you know, I'd tackle that nightmare all over if it meant falling in love with you again."

Taya's knees weakened at the huskiness in his voice.

She rested her hand flat against his chest, relishing his strength. Her diamond wedding set glimmered in the light and she soaked in the thrill of being Dr. Taya Stryker. Keegan's wife.

Her heart bubbled to overflowing with love for her husband. Her hero, champion and defender had also become her best friend and partner.

"Why do you look so serious?"

She smiled. "I was just thinking about how much I love you."

"Well, don't let me stop you." He kissed her.

Taya's cell phone rang, interrupting their kiss, and she pulled away to answer.

"This is Jackson Beaumont, director of the FBI Anthropology department. I'm calling to offer you employment as lead anthropologist."

Taya sucked in a breath. She tried to keep her tone nonchalant. "Thank you, sir." She disconnected and faced Keegan. "I got the job!"

Keegan whooped. "That's outstanding! I'm so proud of you."

The doorbell rang, pulling them apart.

"You know, if these interruptions don't stop, we may have to go back to honeymooning in Jamaica," Keegan threatened, peering through the peephole. "It's my parents, I didn't know they were coming," he whispered.

Taya loved the Strykers. They were warm and kind, taking her into their fold from their first meeting. "We have a lifetime together. Tonight, let's enjoy the blessing of family and maybe next year, we'll have our own little addition to welcome."

* * * * *

*If you enjoyed this story, look for
these other books by Sharee Stover:*

Secret Past
Silent Night Suspect
Untraceable Evidence

Dear Reader,

I hope you enjoyed Taya and Keegan's story. I had so much fun researching this book while eating kolaches.

Taya is strong and confident on the outside. Inside, she struggles with her fears. Keegan encourages her to overcome her fears with the help of God.

Is there a situation you've struggled to face on your own? Friend, know that God is with you always and you can trust Him to get you through.

I love hearing from readers. Let's stay in touch! Please join my newsletter list at www.shareestover.com.

Blessings to you,
Sharee

COMING NEXT MONTH FROM
Love Inspired Suspense

Available December 1, 2020

TRUE BLUE K-9 UNIT: BROOKLYN CHRISTMAS
True Blue K-9 Unit: Brooklyn
by Laura Scott and Maggie K. Black
K-9 officers face danger and find love in these two new holiday novellas. An officer and his furry partner protect a police tech specialist from a stalker who will do anything to get to her, and a K-9 cop and a former army corporal must work together to take down a drug-smuggling ring.

DEADLY AMISH REUNION
Amish Country Justice • by Dana R. Lynn
Jennie Beiler's husband was supposed to be dead, so she's shocked when he rescues her from an attacker. Although Luke has no memories of his *Englisch* wife, now his Amish hometown is their only safe haven from a vengeful fugitive.

CHRISTMAS PROTECTION DETAIL
by Terri Reed
When a call from a friend in trouble leads Nick Delaney and Deputy Kaitlin Lanz to a car crash that killed a single mother, they become the baby's protectors. But can they figure out why someone is after the child...and make sure they all live to see Christmas?

ALASKAN CHRISTMAS TARGET
by Sharon Dunn
With her face splashed across the news after she saves a little boy's life, Natasha Hale's witness protection cover is blown. Now she must rely on Alaska State Trooper Landon Defries to stay one step ahead of a Mafia boss if she hopes to survive the holidays and receive a new identity.

CHRISTMAS UP IN FLAMES
by Lisa Harris
Back in Timber Falls to investigate a string of arsons, fire inspector Claire Holiday plans to do her job and leave...until her B&B is set on fire while she's sleeping. Can she team up with firefighter Reid O'Callaghan—her secret son's father—to catch the serial arsonist before her life goes up in flames?

ARCTIC CHRISTMAS AMBUSH
by Sherri Shackelford
After discovering her mentor has been murdered, Kara Riley becomes the killer's next target—and her best chance at survival is Alaska State Trooper Shane Taylor. Trapped by a snowstorm, can they find the culprit before he corners Kara?

———————

LOOK FOR THESE AND OTHER LOVE INSPIRED BOOKS WHEREVER BOOKS ARE SOLD, INCLUDING MOST BOOKSTORES, SUPERMARKETS, DISCOUNT STORES AND DRUGSTORES.

LISCNM1120

Get 4 **FREE REWARDS!**

We'll send you 2 FREE Books plus 2 FREE Mystery Gifts.

Love Inspired Suspense books showcase how courage and optimism unite in stories of faith and love in the face of danger.